Walking at
Sea Level

SCEPTRE

Also by Richard Kearney

Fiction

Sam's Fall

Non-Fiction

Poétique du Possible
Dialogues with Contemporary Continental Thinkers
Myth and Motherland
Modern Movements in European Philosophy
Transitions: Narratives in Modern Irish Culture
The Wake of Imagination
Poetics of Imagining
Angel of Patrick's Hill
Visions of Europe
Poetics of Modernity
States of Mind
Postnationalist Ireland

Edited by Richard Kearney

Heidegger et la Question de Dieu
The Black Book: On Third Level Education
The Irish Mind: Exploring Intellectual Traditions
The Crane Bag Book of Irish Studies, Volume 1
The Crane Bag Book of Irish Studies, Volume 2
Across the Frontiers: Ireland in the 1990s
Migrations: The Irish at Home and Abroad
Les Métamorphoses de la Raison Herméneutique
Continental Philosophy in the Twentieth Century
Paul Ricoeur: The Hermeneutics of Action
The Continental Philosophy Reader
Questioning Ethics

Walking at Sea Level

RICHARD KEARNEY

SCEPTRE

First published in Great Britain in 1997 by Hodder and Stoughton
A division of Hodder Headline PLC
A Sceptre Book

10 9 8 7 6 5 4 3 2 1

A CIP catalogue record for this book is
available from the British Library.

ISBN 0 340 62819 7

Typeset by Palimpsest Book Production Limited,
Polmont, Stirlingshire
Printed and bound in Great Britain by
Mackays of Chatham PLC, Chatham, Kent

Hodder and Stoughton
A division of Hodder Headline PLC
338 Euston Road
London NW1 3BH

For Anne Bernard and Susan Brown

'They come to such presumption that some say they are even stronger than the Christ . . . Jesus, they say, spoke in a mystery to his disciples privately, and charged them to hand these things on to those who assented . . . They practise magic arts and incantations, love potions and love-feasts, familiar spirits and dream-inducers. They live a dissipated life and hold an impious doctrine and use the name as a cloak for their wickedness. So abandoned are they in their recklessness that they claim to be able to practise anything whatsoever that is ungodly and impious, for conduct is only good and evil, they say, in the opinion of men . . . They call themselves gnostics.'

St Irenaeus on the Carpocratians,
Against Heresies, 1.25.1–6, AD 190

PART I

∫

Dear Jack

*I have to leave Geneva and I can't take Emilie with me.
Mother has offered to look after her, but I think the person she
needs most right now is you, her father. Something has happened which I can't explain yet but which changes everything.
I see things now I never saw before. This isn't easy for Emilie.
She doesn't understand why I have to leave so suddenly and
why I can't tell her where I'm going. She's confused, though
excited, at the possibility of seeing you again after all this time.
It has been five years, but she hasn't forgotten.*

*I've thought a lot before asking you to return like this. I can't
say anything more just now but I believe this is right and trust
you will come.*

Raphaëlle

MONTREAL

'Where can I flee from your presence?'

Psalm 139

White flakes dissolved against the window of the tutors' room. Jack Toland looked down on to Sherbrooke Street from his fifth-floor office, his forehead pressed to the cold pane. Outside, Montrealers hurried along the slippery pavements, pulling their long coats about them as they prepared for the last snowstorm of the season. He loosened his collar and cursed the university heating system. 'Stifling,' he said to himself, tugging his shirt up from his trousers, crumpled and baggy enough around the knees to mask the brace on his right leg.

What was Raphaëlle doing, he thought, calling him back to Geneva after all this time? A letter – 'out of the blues', as she used to say in her odd English – asking him to come home and play father to a child who mightn't even remember what he looked like.

He hooked his walking stick over the radiator by the window and found himself trying to summon up an image of his daughter. He couldn't recall Emilie's birth, of course, since he hadn't been there for it. Recovering from a drug overdose and a dozen ankle stitches in the Clinique Générale in Geneva, he hadn't learned of Emilie's existence, or her name, until the day after she'd been born. The week before the birth he'd had a nightmare – Raphaëlle making love to his late brother, Sam. Both of them clutching each other under water, air bubbles billowing from open mouths, their hair waving upwards like bootlace weed. Jack had sat up in bed sweating and had woken Raphaëlle and asked her who was the father of the child inside her. She had put her hand to her huge tummy and told him then, as she had so many times since: he – Jack – was the father. She had never made love with Sam. He wanted to believe her, but how could he ever really tell? Not from the baby's eyes or mouth or chin. He and Sam were twins.

So, on the eve of Emilie's birth, they'd rowed and Jack had gone on his first serious binge. It had started with heavy drinking at a drug-seller's bedsit near the Plaine de Plainpalais, followed by a cocktail of hallucinogens that had exploded in his brain and made him so manic that the peddler's dog had attacked him and bitten right into his dead leg. Canine incisions through the calf, sundered ligaments. Jack hadn't felt a thing, but needed twelve stitches.

He screwed his eyes tight and butted his forehead several times against the thick pane. His own daughter entering life in one Geneva hospital while he was having a limb sutured in another.

He removed his jacket and folded it over the back of his chair and took a pile of books from the shelf. Volumes by his seventeenth-century namesake, John Toland of Donegal. He scanned the spine of each edition before slotting them into a canvas bag. They were old, with scuffed leather covers, and included some early editions published in Dublin in the 1720s. He read every title out loud, slowly and deliberately. He loved lists. *Letters to Serena. Amyntor. Pantheisticon. Tetradymus. An Appeal to Honest People against Wicked Priests. A Defence of Mr Toland in a Letter to Himself. Vindicius Liberius. Anglia Libera. Nazarenus. Christianity Not Mysterious.* He lingered over the last volume, reciting the full title and subtitle aloud. *Christianity Not Mysterious: or a Treatise showing that there is nothing in the Gospel contrary to Reason, nor above it: and that no Christian Doctrine can be properly called a Mystery.* He smelled the title page, then bent down and placed the book in the holder on his desk.

'You're taking all those?' said a voice from behind. Danièle Deguy, Jack's fellow physics tutor, had entered the office. She rolled her eyes to heaven and dropped into a swivel chair at the other desk.

He worked the zip of his bag and nodded. He did not look up.

'They've libraries in Geneva too,' said Danièle, leaning back in her seat, folding one long leg over another.

'I don't like libraries. I like my own copies – with my own marks in them.' He balanced a book in either hand.

'You're going to look after your daughter, not defend your thesis. Couldn't you leave this behind for a while?'

'Not now, I'm at the crucial bit.'

'You're always at the crucial bit!'

'I can't just drop it . . .'

'You dropped your family when it suited you.' Danièle flashed brown eyes at him.

'You know nothing of that,' said Jack. He stood up straight, releasing the canvas handles.

'Because you never let me know.' Danièle's voice wavered a little, then grew hard. 'You're like a shellfish, all shut in.'

Jack looked down at his shoes and hissed an inaudible curse. It was true he'd hardly spoken of his former life since he'd moved to Montreal. The day he'd left Raphaëlle and Emilie behind in Geneva was the last day he'd seen them – 19 September 1984. He had tried desperately, during the first months after the split, to make amends, repair the hurt, to win back Raphaëlle and Emilie by any means he could – letters, telegrams, telephone calls. But the scar was too deep. Throughout his five long years in Montreal their absence haunted him, as if a war were being waged somewhere inside him between hope and doubt, between the will to remember and the will to forget. Until the two sides cancelled each other out. Oblivion the mind's own morphine. It seemed extraordinary, now that he thought about it, now that he had to think about it. But he couldn't actually *see* their faces. Not Raphaëlle's. Not Emilie's. They were as spectral as his own leg.

He closed his eyes. Nothing. Opening his eyes again after a few moments, he gazed out at the high-rise Montreal roofs slicing a flinty sky, and tried to recall the first moments Emilie learned to walk, to speak, to swim, to draw, to write. Her first day at kindergarten. Her first birthday. But no images came. It was only as he turned from the snow-flecked window and shuffled back towards his desk that a single memory of his daughter returned, unbidden – an irate little face screaming at him as it emerged from a drift of snow. Chamonix, February 1983. Their last skiing outing *en famille*. Emilie had skidded as she tried to come to a halt before him on tiny skis at the foot of the learning slope. Jack was sitting on a chair under a pine tree and didn't have the reflexes to reach out and break her fall. He had watched Emilie glide towards him in slow motion, then slip on the grooved ice, a gloved hand held out as he just sat there, clamped to his chair, leaden and dazed, unable to do anything but stare at his four-year-old daughter slewed up to her waist in snow, her head flaked with tiny, glisting crystals. He had loved her then with an intensity approaching pain.

Jack turned his head towards Danièle who was still staring at him, one arm resting on the side of her chair. Her eyes were the colour of dark wood. 'Did you ring your mother-in-law about your time of arrival?'

'I did,' he replied.

'And she didn't say anything more about your wife?'

'No. She says she can't talk about that until I meet her tomorrow.' Jack turned his back to Danièle as he reached over to his duffel coat hanging by the door. He took a tan pouch from his pocket and some Rizla papers. Spreading tangled shreds of marijuana on to the light paper curled in his hand, he rolled it, slid his tongue along the edge and twisted the top. Then, balancing the joint between his pursed lips, he lit up, sucking long scoops of smoke into his lungs. He looked at Danièle sitting at her cluttered desk, frowning, as he stood there immobile for several seconds, inhaling, exhaling, like a fish in an aquarium suspended on wimpling fins, going nowhere. Nothing else existed at that moment but that close, mute, airless space.

'If you're going, we'd better go,' Danièle said after a while.

OK, Jack nodded wetting thumb and forefinger with his tongue and putting out the joint. He picked up his bag and they left the office.

2 ∫

Danièle helped Jack carry his bag towards the elevator of
the Bronfman building. They held one strap each, having
the air of old acquaintances as they leaned in opposite
directions to balance the load between them. They walked
with measured steps, each footfall punctuated by the click
on the corridor of Jack's favourite stick, a blackthorn given
to him by his late father. They passed the noticeboards
bristling with timetables for end-of-term exams in Theoretical and Applied Physics. But Jack was concentrating
on Danièle's tall body moving in step beside him. Those
graceful high-diver legs, that elegant spine and strong neck.
Danièle, friend, colleague and occasional lover, who would
take his last four classes for him and grade the undergrad
papers after he'd gone.

The elevator took a long time to arrive. There were
plenty of students about, looking for mid-term marks.
Some stepped aside to let Jack pass as he leaned heavily
on his stick, exaggerating his infirmity. He knew the power
of the gammy leg. Power of the powerless, never failed.
Like Philoctetes, the exile with the putrefying foot. Or
other Greek fellows with wounded limbs – Oedipus, Laios,
Labdacos, Chiron. Or non-Greeks like Adonis and the Fisher
King. Or one-legged seamen like Ahab and John Silver.
Lists. Jack was a devil for lists.

As the lift clanked towards them on the fifth floor,

Jack rubbed the bridge of his nose and thought about his unfinished thesis. He was still deciding on a title. He inventoried the possibilities. *The Life and Times of J.J. Toland* – too populist. *Reasons of a Rationalist: Who was Janus Junius Toland?* – too gimmicky. *Towards a Radical Enlightenment: The Case of John Toland* – too derivative. *Against Mystification: Toland's Critique of Religious Ideology* – too cerebral. He buttoned the top of his shirt and straightened his tie. He'd think of something.

Jack knew his department chair was distraught about the delays. The Faculty Committee of Graduate Research had told him he'd get no more teaching if the thesis wasn't completed by the new academic term. At different stages during his five-year research they'd come up with what they deemed more suitable PhD topics: quantum probability of alpha particles penetrating a nucleus; the gravothermal effects of light particles placed in a spherical container; the implications of Einstein's quest for a general theory for alternative modes of spatial measurement; the experimental hypothesis that white holes, unlike black ones, forfeit angular momentum. But Jack would not be deflected. His doctoral work on J.J. Toland's theory of matter was worth ten such projects. He knew the leaps his Donegal namesake made in the history of science, even if no one else did. Leaps so unheralded he had to hide his findings behind coded signs, conceal esoteric implications inside plain statements, like little clawed beasts inside coloured shells. By such strategies of subterfuge, Toland challenged the prejudice of twelve hundred years of Western thought and propagated a knowledge so radical and alarming that, no sooner glimpsed, it was censored and condemned.

Countless times over the years, Jack had sought to persuade his McGill professors that J.J. Toland had discovered things few before him dared to contemplate – that God is matter, that matter is motion, that motion is a vortex. If dictionaries of science listed him at all, they did so in footnotes to Locke, Leibniz, Bruno or Spinoza. They understood nothing of the *real* Toland. The man who declared Universal Space to be the locus of absolute knowledge – a truth unutterable in Christendom since Augustine inveighed against materialist visions of space in the fifth century. Book six of the *Confessions* put paid to that for centuries. Until Toland lifted the lid and let the genie of reason rise once more into the skies of the Western universe.

The lid was lifted surreptitiously, of course. It had to be, Jack explained to his faculty committee, if Toland was to avoid being hanged. That's why he used pseudonyms and esoteric arguments. A matter of survival, so ingenious that most of his intellectual contemporaries also fell for his ploys. Locke and Newton were taken in. Leibniz and Berkeley too. And now, in 1989, Jack's own faculty committee of ultra-conservatives. In spite of his repeated arguments, sitting before the review board, explaining each twist of his deliberations step by meticulous step, the professors replied that no faculty of science, no matter how theoretical, could tolerate such unsupported hypotheses. Jack was way offside, they warned. What he was doing was philosophy, not physics. But Jack didn't care. He was right; they were wrong. He knew J.J. Toland was more than a curious namesake neglected by history. Much more. He knew what everyone ignored – except for his dead twin, Sam, and their abbot at Columbanus Abbey – that Toland was one of Europe's greatest minds. The first enlightened thinker to declare that God was space.

There were still gaps in Toland's story; Jack knew that. Just as there were gaps in his own. But he'd get to the bottom of things. He'd complete the portrait his dead brother had only been able to begin, he'd find the reasons within reasons that made Toland a revolutionary rationalist. He'd set the legend straight and tell it as it was once and for all.

The elevator arrived, its double metal doors sliding open

with a whoosh. Jack shuffled into the crowded space after Danièle. He stroked the rusty stubble on his chin and remembered he'd forgotten to shave. His stomach sank as he descended to the ground floor. Out on Sherbrooke, he pulled his collar up to his throat and swallowed. There was a bitter wind gusting down McTavish Avenue and the pavements were already glistening with sleet. No birds. No leaves. No trees. He waited there, bag at his feet, as Danièle took a short cut to the campus carpark through the Redpath tunnel. Jack watched as she traversed the grassy quad facing the copper domes of Burnside Hall. Within an hour that yellow lawn, and the green domes above it, would be shrouded in white sheets.

To keep warm, he paced back and forth, marking out a hopscotch of traces in the snow. He toed his bag with his right foot. 'Time to go,' he said aloud, his breath making aqueous balloons in the air. He sniffed, smelling stale smoke on his own breath, and peered down Sherbrooke. Still no sign of Danièle's car. His stick ferreted after flecks of snow melting on the pavement. With his free hand he fished in his jacket for tobacco and cursed. He'd left it in the office. He looked up but dipped his head again almost immediately, shading his eyes from the spray of sleet that fell from the sky.

He turned and leaned his back into the wind. His good foot was beginning to feel the cold. He tapped it on the pavement repeatedly as if it were a pedal. Still no sign of the car and the traffic was thickening by the minute. What in the name of Jesus was Raphaëlle doing summoning him back to look after Emilie? He struck the ground hard with his stick. The old pet fear. The black worm curled in the pit of his soul was beginning to stir again. He could sense its snub-nosed, eyeless head rising up inside him. The doubt that destroyed everything. Why could he never believe Raphaëlle? Why could he never really trust her? Not then, not now? He turned his head back into the pelting snow and cursed again to the son of God.

Danièle's rusting yellow Volkswagen pulled in at last and double-parked. Jack walked forward, bag in hand. A lustrous film of snow powder had formed in front of the Bronfman building, protected from the north wind. Jack almost slipped on it but righted himself, crouching to deliver his bag to Danièle. Then he was in, snug in the passenger seat, waving *au revoir*, for now at any rate, to the campus he'd worked in for five years of his life.

3

Neither spoke much as they drove through heavy traffic to Jack's apartment on rue Bernard. They turned up Parc, passed the Mont Royal monument on the left, and within minutes were swinging into the sprawling francophone suburb of Outremont: 2105 rue Bernard.

Once in the door, Jack went straight to the hall cupboard and began to pull down some old cases from a high shelf. Danièle collapsed on the blue couch in the main room, reached into her leather shoulder bag and took out a small canvas purse. She turned it upside down and shook it like a salt cellar, emptying the contents on to the seat cushion. Amphetamines, uppers and a gram of speed. She checked her watch and spread a thin line of speed on the back of her hand. She tilted her head and inhaled the white powder brusquely through one nostril. Jack turned, watched her, then turned back; he hadn't touched anything but grass since he came to Montreal.

They made love on the floor. Afterwards, Danièle lay beside him, the palms of her hands stretched back behind her head like splayed starfish, a pungent aroma of sex still in the air, the tiny blue naevi beneath her left eyelid beaded with sweat. Lovely, thought Jack, his head bent towards her. She turned over as he reached out a hand and ran it along her bottom and back. 'Hot,' he said; she nodded. Then, propping himself on one arm, Jack leant down to her ankles and feet. 'Cold.' She nodded again. One half hot, the other cold.

Danièle was always like that after sex. *Thermically dysfunctional*. Jack's term. They'd become lovers, off and on, after they'd met in the campus canteen the first week Danièle entered the grad programme, almost two years ago now. Jack had always known there was something about his paralysis that attracted her, something she missed with other men, the space to get in touch with her own desire, losing control without fully losing it, encountering the surprise of her own want like a figure in the dark. He knew because she was the kind of person who spoke about such things. Jack wasn't; but he never gave her any illusions. It hadn't taken long for her to learn that if Jack had lovers from time to time, there was only one woman in his life and that was the woman he refused to speak about. Raphaëlle.

He got to his feet and started to wander about. He served himself a large glass of rye from the side table and, still naked, began taking Toland books from his canvas holdall, stacking them neatly along the inside of an open case. Danièle dressed quickly, watching him.

'You really should give up on Toland,' she said, stretching. 'He's not worth the candle.'

Jack didn't respond. He put another volume into the case, inspecting the title on the spine as he did so.

'Why waste more time on him?' She stood before a mirror by the entrance, adjusting her loose hair and blouse.

'He was unique.' Jack rested a hand on the upper lid of the case. 'And we have the same name.'

'Like thousands of people in the telephone book.' She shrugged her shoulders.

Jack went on packing.

'It's so irrelevant!' Danièle spun on her heels and clapped her hands impatiently. 'J.J. Toland was a fraud.'

'You just don't get it, do you,' said Jack. 'He was a genius *pretending* to be a fraud . . .'

'A double fake, then, a two-timer?' Her words had an edge to them.

'Someone with a message people like you can't take.'

'But of course!' She put the back of her hand to her forehead and rolled her eyes upwards. 'Divinity is space! Knowledge is matter! The universe is absolute!' She turned away and shrugged. 'I know your damn thesis by heart.'

'But you still don't *understand* what Toland actually meant.'

'If I don't, it's for a good reason – he never *said* what he meant.'

'And you know why. His first book almost saw the end of him. He didn't want to die.'

Danièle put her hands to her hips. 'So he lied to survive. Sure. And that makes him great?'

Jack weighed a volume in one hand, stroking the scar along his hip with the other. He rounded on her. 'I know it's hard for you New Worlders to appreciate anything approximating history. But think for a moment what it was like for a Gaelic-speaking Catholic like Toland, born at the arse-end of Europe at the end of the seventeenth century.' He tapped the spine of the book. 'The only way to get on was to change his religion and his name . . .'

'To John John Toland.' She pointed to the name on the cover.

'Janus Junius in Latin, John John in English.'

'To pass himself off as a gent!'

'With good cause.'

'To take the mystery out of matter – which he never quite got round to.' She took up one of Jack's books and sat forward on the sofa.

'Which took some time.' Jack held an open palm towards the book and Danièle handed it back to him.

'Five years?' She arched an eyebrow and folded her arms.

'All his life.' Jack let the Toland volume drop gently into
the case with a flip of his wrist. He then reached for his
trousers on the sofa and began to pull them on. 'Of course,
he had to go incognito, especially after his book was burnt
by Parliament. He's even rumoured to have withheld some
of his own writings.'

'You never told me that.'

'I never told you lots of things.' He placed another book in
his case. He leaned back again. 'But that's a fact – discretion
was survival. Toland even served as an agent in Hanover
and taught Queen Sophie Charlotte of Prussia his secret
theory of the vortex . . .'

'Ah yes, let me see,' she pondered, hand to chin, 'a mass
of swirling fluid swallowing all that approaches.'

'Good memory.' He adjusted his trouser belt and slipped
a vest over his head.

'I've had practice.' She slipped off the arm of the sofa.
'But I still don't forgive Toland: for a freethinker he wasn't
very free with his thought.'

Jack crouched down and began to strap on his calliper.
'I've told you a thousand times, had Toland spoken out he'd
have been hanged.'

'And if caught in Queen Sophie's bed?'

'That's another story.'

'Another loose Irishman, by the sounds of it.'

'*Aithníonn ciaróg ciaróg eile*,' said Jack, clicking his knee-
clasp with a snap.

Danièle threw him a quizzical look.

'Gaelic,' he explained. 'One of Toland's Donegal maxims.
It takes a black beetle to know one.'

'You're all caught up with each other, you Irish. You're
like fish swimming about in an aquarium. You never look
out, the glass is all fogged up, and no one changes the
water.'

Jack grinned at her. He loved it when he riled her. He
picked up his pullover and tugged it over his head; it smelled

of stale marijuana, heavy and sweet. Fully dressed again, he ambled towards a large chest of drawers at the other end of the sitting room, and proceeded to remove some clothes for his journey.

4

Jack watched Danièle as she left the room and made her way towards the tiny kitchen. Though they had known each other for two years, she'd rarely been inside his flat. Now that he was about to leave he felt somewhat guilty about his furtiveness, almost regretting he hadn't shared more of his pain at losing Raphaëlle and Emilie, his sense of shame about what had happened.

From his standing position by the chest of drawers, he observed her stepping briskly over papers and grade sheets, passing a row of potted plants and pygmy trees skirting the length of the corridor, each with a tiny stick and name tag. *Primula, Scilla, Aeonium, Puschkinia, Begonia, Iris, Alfalfa, Narcissus.* The Latin names Jack loved almost as much as his Toland titles. He wondered if she would recite them to herself as she turned into the kitchen, or if she'd stop to admire his favourite specimens from the bonsai nursery and his cherished batch of succulents with fleshy leaves and squat stems – *Elephant Bush, Sedum, Dwarf Daffodil, Grape Hyacinth, African Violet;* and especially the *Portulacaria afra* with its crimson pistils brazenly exposed, as teeming and jewelled as its English name – *Flaming Katy* – inscribed in Jack's meticulous copperplate beneath the Latin.

He wished he'd tidied the kitchen the previous evening, or opened the window to banish the habitual odours of cooking fat, onions and gone-off milk. He regretted having left two tickets for *Arturo Ui* at the Théâtre des Quatre Sous on the door of the fridge, as Danièle would know the second one wasn't for her. But it was too late now. Too late for other regrets as well. Like the other times he'd cheated on her. Hardly a month after their first night out in the Bibloquet, he was discovered by Danièle sleeping with a sophomore student, a pretty New Age blonde who used words like 'limerence' and 'anahedonoidal' in her essays and was so obsessed with the hole in the ozone layer that she never removed her sunglasses. Danièle had talked to her in the McGill canteen and quickly realised that Jack had sent her the same note after her first night. *I leave you my words so that you will have my presence all the days and nights we are absent from each other . . .*

Jack winced at the memory. Worse still was the card he had sent Danièle for her twenty-fifth birthday. A picture postcard of a Degas nude brushing her hair over a bent head with a rousing inscription in Jack's hand on the back: 'You put my blindness to flight. You shed your fragrance about me; I drew breath and now I gasp for your sweet odour. I tasted you, and now I hunger and thirst for you. You touched me, and I am inflamed with love.' A loose translation, Jack had claimed, of an ancient Tunisian love poet; and Danièle had believed him, until a few months later she had come across the passage marked in ink in Jack's copy of St Augustine's *Confessions* in their office. Her birthday poem, she was horrified to discover, was lifted straight from Book ten of the Saint's panegyric to God the Father!

But there was more between them than sex. There was science. And science was what really mattered. Jack had no doubt about that. It was as much of a passion for her as for him. Danièle would get her degree and get to the top. Though she'd changed her topic after the first semester – from the study of gravitational torcs in the precession of equinoxes to the problem of radiation in strong fields –

she was already on to her third chapter. Science was their shared obsession and they spent most of their time together teaching it or talking about it. They'd co-taught physics modules to freshers twice a week at 9 a.m. for the last two terms. They'd double-marked undergrad exams, read each other's papers and chatted about respective projects into the early hours of the morning. In those late-night talks, they'd spent hours discussing the missing link in Toland's theory of matter, tirelessly debated black holes, and indulged in endless wild fantasies about the fourth dimension – that elusive immensity of space surpassing the three known dimensions and eternalising itself in all directions. They'd laughed a lot too, and smoked dope and got as high as kites on bottles of their favourite Rigorello. Until it almost seemed as if they'd known each other forever, and Danièle would ask about Ireland or Geneva, or Raphaëlle or Emilie or Sam, or how Jack had maimed his leg – and Jack would recoil in an instant, go dark and cranky and say he didn't want to speak about his past. And once he'd snapped so fiercely that Danièle had cried and asked him to leave her flat and they hadn't talked for weeks. He'd apologised, of course, but after that they agreed that if they were to be friends there was to be no past. They even agreed the sex was a sideshow, a scatter of momentary and enjoyable lapses. They got on better then, and shared a grad office for four semesters without once squabbling.

Jack was in the bathroom shaving when Danièle returned to the living room carrying two cups of steaming liquid. He watched her through the open door as she looked about for a surface on which to place the tea and hummed Roch Voisine's recent hit. The large case was open on the couch, almost full now, with a photo lying on top of some shirts. Danièle rested the cups on the arm of the couch and took the photograph from the case. She held it close to her face, then took a step closer to the window to get a better look. Jack wondered what she was thinking as she scrutinised every detail. Raphaëlle's first photo of Jack and Sam. Jack looking half his present age, standing in front of a forest beside Sam – just like Jack but slighter, paler, in monk's robes, a shade in his eyes. Jack stood by the bathroom door gazing at Danièle as she turned the photo over in her hands and read the caption: *For Jack, remembering our first visit together to Columbanus Abbey, love Raphaëlle.*

She replaced the photo in the case but said nothing as Jack returned to the room with his towel and washbag. As he finished his packing and zipped up his case, she went to the window, flecked with tiny paws of snow, and stared across at the chapel of Grégoire L'Illuminateur opposite, which stood in shy isolation from the other red-brick apartments on the block, its apex roof like a white tin hat.

'Let's go,' she said after a few minutes. 'I'll take this.' She reached down to one of Jack's cases.

'I can manage,' he protested.

'That's what you always say,' she said, grabbing the case anyway and lifting it up.

5

Back in the Volkswagen, Danièle swung full circle on to the gleaming street, heading south to Mirabelle airport. Snow grains, bigger now, were splattering the windshield. It was Saturday evening and a cluster of Hassidic Jews wearing black hats and ringlets were gathered on the corner of Bernard and Parc, outside the local synagogue. Their hands were dug into long coats and they stamped their patent black shoes like tap-dancers to keep their feet warm. Curious, smiled Jack, how J.J. Toland had campaigned to emancipate Jews in eighteenth-century Europe. Wandering tribes knew wandering tribes. *Aithníonn ciaróg ciaróg eile.*

Danièle pressed the accelerator and sped down the wide street, sluicing a pool of sleet towards a group of youngsters outside the Outremont cinema, queuing to see Claude Fournier's *Les Tisserands du Pouvoir*. The kids swayed back like a choreographed line to avoid the spray, but Jack and Danièle didn't notice; their eyes were fixed on the road ahead, turning incandescent before them as the snow cascaded from the skies in a full-blown blizzard.

There was a jam on Parc. Jack fidgeted with the cane clamped between his knees; Danièle hummed Lavoie's '*Je veux voir New York*' slightly off tune. North-westerly gusts stirred whirlpools of snow dust up from the pavement. Then they were through, a straight run to Mirabelle.

Outside the Swissair terminal, Jack leaned over to kiss her goodbye, but she drew back. In the beggared yellow light he spied the bareness of her long legs bunched under the steering wheel and almost regretted he was leaving. She'd surely park the car, he thought, and help him into the lobby with his luggage. But she didn't. Remaining in the driving seat, she summoned a porter with a semaphore wave and motioned him towards the boot.

'Bye, Jack,' she said, crinkling her eyes towards the rear-view mirror. A taxi was queuing behind to deliver its charge, light flashing, impatient. 'Things can only get better,' she added.

'Sure.' Jack paused, resting his weight on the porter's trolley. He raised a hand and brushed a spangle of melting crystals from his head.

Danièle stayed where she was. No embrace, no handshake, no wave-a-kiss goodbye. Just a farewell nod as she reached across and pulled the door shut behind him.

Jack stepped back on to his stick as she swung the wheel full circle and the car sped off, an amber bubble dissolving into the chalk-flecked dark.

Entering the check-in lounge, he met his reflection in the large vitrine. He'd always trusted mirrors, ever since he was a boy. What he saw looking back at him was a fallen image of his former self. Scarcely a trace of the JFK lookalike who captained the Munster Schoolboys team and made the girls from Laurel Hill swoon with his dashing red hair and big smiling eyes. What he saw in front of him was a slack face, eyes creased and lined around the edges, complexion slightly jaundiced from a cranky liver.

He struggled into Departures with his large case and shoulder bag. The porter held the door, then closed it quickly to keep the gusts out.

A long queue confronted him, snaking its way towards the counter where officials were conversing. He checked his watch; he doubted the line could be cleared before departure. Then a serene voice announced that all flights were suspended owing to storm conditions. Despondent passengers chatted about the worsening weather – eighteen inches of snow expected to fall overnight, temperatures plummeting from fifty-five to thirty degrees, some lines already down on main thoroughfares, emergency teams brought in to defreeze the jets on the runway and man the extra snowploughs. Most people slunk off towards the exits, returning to homes or hotels in the city, but Jack hadn't the heart to join the scramble for taxis and buses. He'd winter out the storm here at the airport, along with a few hundred others. *La nuit sera longue mais elle passera*, he consoled himself – a line from Damiens, the tortured regicide, which Raphaëlle had once quoted to him after one of his lapses.

He headed for the bar, his right leg swinging in small semicircles like a compass needle making curt sweeps. The brasserie sold pizzas, chowder, sushi. But he didn't feel like food. Balancing his blackthorn on the ebony counter, he ordered a double martini straight up.

He swallowed the cocktail and ordered the same again. There was already a lightness in his brain and he could feel his face loosen as the alcohol burned through him. He wanted a joint, but was glad he'd left his supply behind in the office. That was the last thing he needed going through customs. And he didn't feel like arriving in Geneva smelling like a burnt marijuana plant. A TV mounted high on the wall of the bar showed a leather-clad youngster in a black cowboy hat rocking up and down to the beat of electric instruments, his high voice floating lazily through the crowded saloon, repeating the same words over and over. *Outside is America. Outside is America.* ''Fraid not,' said Jack, lifting his glass to the monitor. 'It's Canada.'

He stretched along the counter for a copy of the *Montreal Gazette*, left by another customer, and perused the leads. Mulrooney locked in dispute over federal legislation with

Bourassa in Quebec. An elderly pastor and his wife clubbed to death in their quaint Westmount home by teenagers with baseball bats. A Solar Templar sect outside Quebec suspected of paedophile rites and cult suicide. Feared renewal of an IRA bombing campaign in Britain. Meteorological reports of blizzards curling down from Manitoba and Saskatchewan. But Jack wasn't registering. His eyes were unfocused. His hand went to his smooth-shaved chin.

The last time he'd sat at this counter was with Charmaine Le Monde, the sophomore he'd been two-timing when he met Danièle. He'd taken her to the airport at the end of spring term and they'd sat there drinking for hours, waiting for her delayed plane home to Ottawa. They kept ordering more whiskies and ginger until they both got so randy they decided they'd have a last fling before take-off. They tried the handicapped toilet but it was occupied, so they finally settled for what seemed like a sequestered pillar by the lost luggage office on the ground floor. Jack wrapped his large grey duffel coat around her and they did it standing up against a broad concrete column. A double-backed beast with not a soul in sight. They stared into the dilated pupils of each other's eyes for what seemed like an eternity until someone tapped Jack's shoulder and he swung round to find a uniformed man pointing to a security camera hanging from the ceiling above them.

He grimaced now at the thought of it and finished his second cocktail in a single swallow. The alcohol did its job as usual, blurring the lines between him and his surroundings. He loved this sense of privileged belonging, of being at one with the décor, blessed and bestowed by everything he touched and saw. As if the airport saloon were a stage scene mounted specially for him. As if the space in which he found himself were a proscenium where every line of vision converged on the vanishing point of himself. Whenever he was laced with alcohol, Jack knew with unassailable conviction that if the plane he boarded crashed he would survive; if lost in a forest, every specimen of tree would name itself for him; if marooned at sea, each wave would flow to his embrace; if grounded on a mountain every valley would radiate beneath his gaze.

Looking around him now, he relished the certainty that the barman heading towards his empty glass with a bottle of vermouth and a measure of gin had been waiting to perform this service all evening.

He sipped at his replenished cocktail and placed it to one side, then bent down towards his shoulder bag under the bar stool and took out a sheaf of loosely bound notes, laying them open on the counter before him. He always enjoyed his opening note. His face creased into a half-smile as he inclined his head over the pages, his heart skipping a beat as it invariably did whenever he reread his own work. The sheer nerve of his hypothesis never ceased to cheer him – J.J. Toland, the great unacknowledged rationalist of the Enlightenment. Not a sentence too many, although it was almost eighteen months since he'd added a new one.

Toland on ice – with a good dash of gin. The most effective antidote to his anxieties. The perfect mix which never failed to fill the gap, to salve the pain whenever he thought of Raphaëlle, or couldn't bear to think of her. He reached for his glass with one hand, turning over the first page of his Biographical Introduction with the other.

6 ∫

J.J. Toland was known in his local parish of Inishowen as Eoghan na Leabhair – John of the Books. He soon left his native Donegal, however, and travelled, researched, wrote and conspired through-out a number of Continental cities. Berlin, Hanover, Düsseldorf, Prague, Amsterdam, Leiden, Bern. He knew these cities and their coffee houses knew him. He spoke ten languages and published a hundred books. He changed professions as frequently as he did religions. Working as a linguist and scholar at Oxford in the early part of his life, Toland's main source of income during his later sojourns on the Continent was as pamphleteer, court diplomat and, some suspected, secret agent. In Prussia, he taught science behind closed doors to the Electress Sophia and was rewarded for his exertions, record has it, with 'gold medals and other curiosities to a considerable value'.

During his life, Toland went by various aliases, reclaiming a noble genealogy dating back to Gaelic aristocracy – the Tuathaláin. He even persuaded Irish Franciscans in Prague to certify his story and offer him refuge in their College (called Hybernska to this day). Privately insecure, Toland's public persona was one of bold assertion and extravagant confidence. Especially in matters of science and philosophy. His subtle objections to established views on matter and motion marked a revolutionary challenge; where Newtonians saw motion as external to bodies, Toland saw it as internal; where they claimed objects were discrete, Toland believed that 'every material thing is all things, and all things are but one'.

In the Fifth Letter to Serena he outlined his materialist vision thus: 'All the parts of the universe are in constant motion of destroying and begetting, of begetting and destroying; and the greater systems are acknowledged to have their ceaseless movements as well as the smallest particles, the very central globes of the vortexes turning about their own axes; and every particle in the vortex gravitating towards the centre.'

What exactly Toland was no one has yet been able to say. His enemies, who were legion, dismissed him with a variety of slurs – pantheist mytagogue, pseudo-Spinozist, crypto-hylozoist, plagiarist of Locke and Bayle, clandestine disciple of Bruno, intellectual pirate and polemicist. Who knew the truth about Toland? Perhaps Toland himself confided to someone during a drunken spree in some Continental coffee house. Perhaps his 'profane and loose ways' did, as the Earl of Shaftesbury warned, make it impossible for anyone to know when he was serious. Or perhaps his fellow countryman, Father Sheils, was right when he declared: 'Ní fear a labhras ach an Diabhal' *('Tis not a man who speaks but the Devil!).*

Perhaps. But it is my considered view, having researched and reviewed the available literature, including primary and secondary sources, that J.J. Toland was a thoroughgoing rationalist behind all the guises – a freethinker unable to speak his name for fear of mortal retribution, a deconstructor avant la lettre *of mysteries and mystifications, of lies and illusions, of cover-ups and subterfuge. If anyone brought the modern method of doubt to its logical extreme, it was Toland. Master of suspicion* par excellence, *he proved more radical than all his fellow rationalists – Descartes, Spinoza, Leibniz, Locke. Of that, if only that, there is no doubt.*

Toland was a rationalist of many traits – cosmopolitan before his time, hermeneut of scriptures, enlightened republican, a forerunner of revolution reviled in most polite society across Europe. An impolitic genius so censured in his time that another Irishman, Edmund Burke, could ask in 1790: 'Who, born within the last forty years, has read one word of Toland . . . ?'

Impecunious for most of his life, Toland enjoyed a spell of wealth from his speculations in New World stocks – conniving with a fellow Irishman from Kerry, Richard Cantillon (hailed by Marx as the founder of political economy). Toland lost his money in the South Sea Bubble, double-crossed, it appears, by an accomplice.

Toland died a pauper in Grub Street, London, in 1722. He signed his last work, Pantheisticon, *with what he claimed was his real name, Janus Junius Edganesius, indicating his place of birth in Inishowen peninsula in the north of Ireland. Beside this name, Toland added the pseudonym,* Cosmopoli – *'one who belongs to the world'. His private and public personae jostled shoulders to the end. Native and internationalist hand in glove. Toland's readers were by this time so accustomed to his stratagems that they took it as one more pseudonymous ruse. As, no doubt, Toland intended. The epitaph on his tombstone in Putney declared he would rise again – but never the same Toland.* Ad idem futurus Tolandus nunquam. *But who was the 'same' Toland?*

'Mind if I borrow a cigarette?'

Jack turned to find a small man, pale and plain, sitting two stools down from him at the bar, staring dumbly, obviously drunk. He pointed to Jack's pack of cigarettes on the counter.

Jack nodded permission and was about to return to his biographical note when the man said, 'Must be some read – the way you've been stuck in like that.'

Jack pretended he hadn't heard. He reached for his cocktail and drained it in one go, placing the glass back on the counter beside his packet of smokes.

'Pleased to meet you.' The man craned his head forward, laughing, a bony hand held out towards Jack. 'My name is Maurice. Maurice Hughes.'

Jack had little choice but to take the man's hand. 'Jack Toland,' he replied, shielding his eyes from the glare of the overhead spots.

'Irish?'

'Yes.'

'I can tell by the accent. And the reddy hair.' He patted his own head.

'Oh.' Jack sniffed. 'Yes.'

'So, what're you reading?'

'Something about a scientist.' Jack did not look up.

'Bit of a scientist myself.' Hughes grinned. He scratched the lobe of his ear. 'Computer science, to be exact.'

'Hard or soft?' asked Jack.

'Hard as it comes,' said Hughes, jerking his neck.

'I did my primary degree in physics and botany,' said Jack. 'Cork University. Late seventies.' He ordered another drink, gesturing to the barman with an inclination of his head. 'Now I'm doing doctoral work on this Irish scientist John John Toland.' He tapped his fingers on the page in front of him.

'Same name as yourself.'

'Almost.'

'Coincidence, no?'

'I call it serendipity.' Jack pulled hard on his cigarette, drawing the smoke down deep into his lungs. His head was beginning to race from the liquor and nicotine and he was suddenly almost relieved to have this perfect stranger to talk to. 'It was the abbot at our school who first told me and my twin brother about him. Sam was my brother's name – he did research on Irish scribes wandering around Europe looking for lost languages. Sam used to love quoting things written by this namesake of ours. And the first time he did it, I actually thought Sam was quoting *me* – I was christened John Toland, you see; Jack's for short.'

'Is that a fact,' said Hughes, wrinkles of amusement fanning out from his eyes.

Jack gave an emphatic nod. 'Half the Jacks in the world are really Johns.'

'Did your brother finish his research?'

Jack shook his head and stared into the bottom of his glass. 'Sam drowned. He was only twenty.'

'I'm sorry.'

'It happened early one morning in a little cove called Poul Gorm, outside Cork. We used to go there every summer.'

'One of my grandparents came from Cork,' said Hughes. He leaned his dish-shaped face towards Jack. His breath smelled of garlic.

Jack pulled back. The stale odour made him swallow hard. He paused, tapping the butt of his cigarette on the shiny counter, then continued. 'After Sam died I became obsessed by this seventeenth-century namesake of ours, as if finding out everything about him, his life, his work, his passion, his thought, his travels, would somehow . . .' He broke off and reached for his glass.

After a few moments' silence, Hughes nodded down towards Jack's typescript. 'Did you find much?'

'Yeah.' Jack sipped his drink.

'Tell me about him.'

'He was born a bastard in Donegal.'

'Good start.'

'His mother was a local whore raped by a vagabond priest.'

'Gets better.'

'His first book made him the talk of Europe at the age of twenty-five.'

'Clever fellow by the sounds of it.'

'He learned fast to protect himself. His ideas were dangerous.'

'Like?'

'Like faith being a lesser form of scientific knowledge.'

'That was dangerous?'

'Of course. In those days, ideas were life and death.' Jack shifted to face Hughes. 'Toland was a rationalist with a price on his head. He had to lie his way to truth. To write in codes and ciphers.' He swirled the martini in his glass, scrutinising the clear liquid. 'But that didn't stop his enemies in London throwing every name they could at him. Infidel, Mahometan, apostate, turncoat, drunk. Even Swift had a go at him – called him an "Irish priest"!'

'Why were they so het up?'

'Because Toland took the mystery out of God. He challenged religion and promised a new kind of knowledge to make all men free. So they sent the hangman after him. To stop him in his tracks.' Jack thumbed through the pages on the counter until his fingers halted at a passage in small print. 'Look. Here. The parliamentary summons.' He read out the words. *'Toland's work to be publicly burnt by the hand of the common hangman.'*

'Is that right!' said Hughes, listing sideways as he tried to read the words himself.

'It is,' said Jack. 'Eleventh September 1697. A terrible day for human reason.'

Hughes nodded gravely several times, then peered down into his empty tankard. After a while he looked up and pointed to Jack's papers. 'Will you publish this stuff?'

'If I finish,' said Jack. He ordered another round. 'I'm not there yet. There are still lots of loose ends, things I can't figure out.' He ran his hand along his scalp. 'I've been working on it now for almost five years, here at McGill, they have a good Toland collection, but I'm still nowhere near finished.'

'So you're taking a break?'

'You could say that.' Jack put his notes back in his shoulder bag and replaced it under his stool. He raised his fresh martini to his lips and sipped slowly. 'I'm actually going back to Geneva to look after my kid daughter.'

'You're a family man?'

'I was. Until my marriage broke up, five years ago, and I came out here to Montreal to work on Toland.'

'You haven't been back in five years?'

'No. The break-up was a bad one. I did some terrible

things.' Jack fingered his glass. 'This stuff didn't help. And there was worse. I was into heavy shit back then.'

'I know all about broken marriages,' said Hughes, launching into a litany of how he'd been through two divorces himself and was now heading for a third and how women should never be trusted, they were all the same. He went on and on, only interrupting himself long enough to take an occasional swallow of beer, until he eventually began to weep and slipped off his stool, fists sunk into his trouser pockets. 'Going to the gents',' he said with a slur. He didn't come back.

The airport bar, its cluttered tables and empty glasses, began to recede as Jack exhaled smoke and spat an olive stone into a cupped hand. A bitter taste stung the back of his throat. His ears crackled. He strained to listen as a lazy voice oozed from the bar's sound system, a song about highways and delta sun and shining cities and Death Valley waters and towers of steel and a woman wandering through a heartland.

> She feels like water in my hand
> Freeway like a river cuts through this land
> Into the side of love like a burning spear
> And the poisonous rain brings a flood of fear . . .

A flood of fear. Yes. Jack rubbed his neck. Moist, slack, slightly unshaven above the Adam's apple. He was on his own now, insupportably alone, in the middle of the night in this over-lit lounge. He sat on for a long while, asking himself over and over what could have got into Raphaëlle to go away like that, and to call him back to Geneva to take care of Emilie? It had to be a man. He remembered his nightmare about Sam and Raphaëlle. And the truth that wasn't a dream. Their secret meeting by the sea, Sam's body dragged from the waves, covered in bladderwrack. Jack's heart thumped and his whole head ached until he couldn't bear to think any more. Leaning on the counter, he cradled his head in the crook of his arm and tumbled into a black sleep.

PART II

She inhaled deep into her body. Keeping her breath there for as long as she could, she inhabited the hush. She could see nothing but a play of black-and-red shadows through closed eyelids. Smell nothing but the fresh perfume from her own clothes. But she could still hear stray noises all around her, the purr of the convex heater by the wall behind her chair, the clatter of someone closing a door at the far end of the corridor, the faint murmur of traffic from the street outside. She listened until these outer noises died away one after another and she could hear only the sound of her own breathing, the air passing in and out of her nostrils, each time holding her breath in longer, pulling it deeper into her body, then letting it flow out from her lungs again in one long whoosh of relief. Yes, she was listening by letting go, coming back down to herself and starting again from where she was. Walking at sea level. Attending. And the further she let go, the more phrases began to return to her, stray snatches of Psalms and Prophets she'd almost forgotten. 'The grass withers, the flower fades . . . Pull yourself up by the roots and plant yourself by the sea . . . Shall not Lebanon in a very little while become a fruitful field and the fruitful field be regarded as a forest . . . Let the sea roar and all that fills it, then shall all the trees of the forest sing for joy . . . There is a river whose streams make glad . . . When you turn to the right or when you turn to the left, your ears shall hear a word behind you saying: 'This is the way, walk in it . . . This is the one who redeems your life from the Pit.'

A long time passed before she opened her eyes. Several bound documents were piled on the morocco leather desktop in front of her. She pressed the switch on the bronze lampstand in the middle of the desk and gazed about her at the terracotta busts perched on three-foot columns marking out the rows of pannelled casements. She looked up at the second-storey gallery of packed volumes with its ornate balcony running from one end of the room to the other. There was nobody. She was on her own, the way she liked it. The air smelled of beeswax polish. She breathed in the clean, sweet odour and reached out for the volumes on her desk, drawing them towards her. She picked up her pen then and held it in the air for several seconds before writing on a large sheet of paper:

God was a Twin. So the Gnostics tell us. Himself and not Himself. Light and dark. He made Adam in his likeness, and Eve from the missing rib of Adam, another mirror image. But these first human twins were not content to be copies; they coveted the secret of creation, the perfect knowledge (gnosis). Adam and Eve wanted to be God. They followed the serpent; and they fell. God too suffered the Fall, co-eternal with his human doubles.

She sat back and raised the print of the Dürer woodcut to eye level. She gazed at it for a long time, then replaced it on the desk and continued to write:

One Fall redeemed by another Fall. Word into flesh. God into Man. The Second Adam. Christ became God's image, Himself and not Himself. But doubles beget doubles as ghosts beget ghosts. Christ had his own image, Thomas the Twin. Thomas comes from thomos, *meaning 'split', and* tu'amu, *meaning 'double'. Thomas is called the 'twin' three times (John 11:16, 20:24, 21:2). He is the doubt haunting Jesus's faith, the darkness shadowing his radiance. The only apostle to touch the Risen Christ, to put his hand into the black gash. Mortal brother reaching into the side of immortal brother – the missing rib of the Second Adam.*

GENEVA

'Direct me in your way and teach me your paths.'
Psalm 25

5

Tufted clouds pocked the sky like puffs of frozen smoke. Halfway over the Atlantic, Jack's nerves were quieting. He peered through the window, his head aching less now after the aspirin the hostess had given him with his meal. He was relieved to be out of Mirabelle. The long wait through the night was over. What he would do when he got to his destination, he wasn't sure. He was going; that was what counted. Matter in motion. He looked out of the window again at the sun's rays slicing a pale strip of sky out on the horizon. And he recalled the verse from Malachi, 'The sun of righteousness shall rise with healing in its wings'. A favourite line of Sam's during his days in Columbanus Abbey.

He didn't feel like finishing his food. *Sole à la Normande*. It smelled good, especially the white wine sauce, but he wasn't hungry. He pushed the tray back and took a pair of earphones from the pouch in front of him, tuning into the news digest on the in-flight channel. It featured, among other things, a mother recovering in a London hospital after giving birth to Siamese twins, delivered by Caesarean section and joined from the breastbone to the navel. Each baby had its own heart and liver, the report explained, but most other organs were fused together. Both babies and mother were said to be stable.

He removed the earphones and sat back, solid in his seat.

The corners of his mouth, like the lines about his eyes, were worn for a man of thirty-one. His head, firm against the headrest, concentrated on some inner motion. He whistled through clenched teeth, an up-down nothing tune. He'd better stop drinking, he thought. For a while anyway. Until he got to know Emilie again and sorted out the Raphaëlle business. A few days on the dry would do him good, his liver too.

He pressed the service button and waited for the hostess. Double whiskey. On the rocks. One for the road – or the sky – whatever. To keep the spirits up, to hold his nerve. Last one. Dutch courage. A man cannot live in the blue without a bottle. He'd read that somewhere.

He put the earphones back on and closed his eyes. A man was screaming 'Love Rescue Me' on the rock channel, so he switched to classical. Glück, 'J'ai perdu mon Eurydice'. Lovely aria, though he couldn't understand why it was sung by a woman. He felt a tap on his shoulder; the hostess had brought his drink. He gave her his tray and took the glass.

Gazing out at the clouds again, the whiskey clasped between his fingers, he felt like a haruspex inspecting skylines for things to come. But it wasn't things to come which came to him. It was things past. The past that never passed. Sam's body drawn from the sea at Poul Gorm, wrapped in kelp as clouds thrashed the sky and waves thumped the rocks. The gleaming coffin carried down the aisle at Columbanus Abbey. Monks intoning verses of the liturgy of St John Chrysostom. Abbot Anselm waving a final benediction. 'Blessed be the soul, wounded in love, for in its wounding it is always healed.' And the other prayer that day which Jack could never forget: 'He whom you love and lose is no longer where he was; he is now wherever you are.'

Other things came back too. Jack's breakdown after Sam's burial, his discovery in Sam's diary that Sam and Raphaëlle had had a secret meeting the night Sam drowned. The black bile. Then the accident. Abbot Anselm's car reversing towards him, Anselm unaware of Jack standing against the wall, cases in hand, on his way to Shannon airport. Screaming out from under the wheels, gripping the wound in his side as Anselm peered helplessly down. Flat on his back then in Limerick hospital for months on end, hip joint smashed, right leg paralysed. Bathing and physio, bars and pulleys, weights and plinths and more besides, until his torso seemed to dwarf his limbs, especially the leg with the scar across the top. Then Anselm leaving for Africa. And the numerous letters to Raphaëlle in Geneva, explaining why he could not travel over; and her replying one day with the news that she could not travel either – that she was pregnant, a difficult pregnancy, forbidden to fly until after the birth. Then Jack's doctors in Limerick recommending a second operation to insert aluminium strips into his fractured hip to restore some mobility to his leg, and eventually taking off from Dublin airport three months and six days after the accident, flying up through the cloudless sky, like a bird released from its cage, wings clipped, legs tagged, but free to gaze down on the Irish Sea the colour of jade and stippled with wind. Returning to Raphaëlle in Geneva. And the wedding and the few happy months before the desperate binges with cocaine and alcohol, starting at Emilie's birth and continuing, on and off, for almost five years – though in between there were good times too, when things came right again for a while and he made promises to Raphaëlle to stop the drugs, to hold down long-term teaching jobs, and it seemed like they'd make it through after all until finally everything fell apart that last terrible night. The night he overdosed while baby-sitting Emilie and she'd gone into hysterics, thinking he was dead. The night Raphaëlle came home to find him lying unconscious on the floor and Emilie kneeling by his side, trembling, her hands trying to press his hand back to life, unable to speak, unable to answer Raphaëlle when she called to her, talked to her, unable to recognise her own mother. That was the night the pin was pulled from the axis of their world and they found themselves revolving through a void.

Returning to Geneva again now, all this came back. Or almost all. Something about Raphaëlle was still missing. Blurred, barred, eclipsed. He could see the outline of her hair and body all right, the contours of her head, but not her features yet. Raphaëlle's full face, her eyes, her nose, her mouth, her voice, her smell, her touch – these still escaped him.

He pressed the overhead buzzer for an attendant and ordered another double Jameson. Stick to the outside, he said to himself. Look out there at the wings of the plane, steady and metallic, smooth and white, humming level over fathomless air. Keep looking out.

2 ∫

Jack slept for several hours then woke with a shiver. He'd
dreamed he was flying back to Europe with Raphaëlle and
Emilie. The plane had crashed into the sea just off the cliffs
of Donegal. He had managed to escape and was waiting
on the rocks for Raphaëlle and Emilie to surface from the
submerged fuselage. Raphaëlle finally emerged from the
waves, dressed in a dripping black dress. Jack took her in his
arms and asked if Emilie had survived. No, said Raphaëlle,
weeping, she had not. She was eating fish when the plane
crashed. Raphaëlle had tried several times to save her from
the sinking vessel but Emilie insisted on finishing her fish.
    Finishing her fish? What did that mean?

When Jack stepped from the plane on to the wet tarmac at Geneva airport, he felt a rush of heat in his dead leg. He knew it was phantom, another trick of his nervous system brought on by the seven hour flight. He was really feeling nothing.

It was raining hard. He held his bag over him with one hand to keep his head dry, and followed the other passengers into Arrivals at a broken pace. He negotiated his strapped limb along the tubular corridor, tilting sideways and back on his stick, the weight of bone and flesh snagging his movement. Quick side-lunging strides, like Ahab walking the tarred deck. Matter in ragged motion. With each laboured step towards the terminal gates, he forced rapid breaths from his mouth.

He stopped at one of the airport boutiques to buy flowers for Belle-Mère. He couldn't decide between red gladioli and white chrysanthemums so he bought both. He took a cab to the city and headed straight to the apartment on rue Richemont. Passing over the Pont du Mont-Blanc, he glimpsed the black waters of Lac Léman turn speckled in the floodlit night, lashed by gusts of rain.

He'd stay off the drink. He would. He'd do it for Emilie.

4 ∫

Raphaëlle's mother answered the door.

'Belle-Mère,' Jack said, calling her what he'd always called her since the day he married Raphaëlle. He handed her the flowers. They shook hands awkwardly.

'*Bonjour*, Jack.' Belle-Mère received him coolly, eyes rheumy with confusion. She held the flowers between them and avoided his gaze. Jack knew she'd never liked him, convinced from the start her daughter was making a mistake. She'd always encouraged Raphaëlle to leave him, until Raphaëlle herself eventually had to concede that things were impossible.

Belle-Mère stood back as Jack entered the hallway, her knit brows still lowered. She didn't ask how he was or if he wanted anything after the flight.

Jack spoke to her in English and she replied in kind, toneless but polite, with her slight Russian inflection. She hadn't changed.

'Where's Emilie?' he asked.

'Asleep. It's late. You'll see her in the morning.'

Jack removed his duffel coat, placed his case by the living-room sofa and faced her. 'Where's Raphaëlle gone?'

Belle-Mère did not flinch. She lifted her head and held his gaze. 'I have no idea.'

'When did you last see her?'

'Eight days ago. The day she went to visit Jean-Pierre

Defay at his family house on the lake by Yvoire. He's her publisher.'

'I know. Is she involved with someone?'

'Not that I'm aware ...' Belle-Mère sat down on a velvet armchair by the window. Her gaze washed over Jack without taking him in. 'She was working on some last-minute prints for her latest book. I had come to take care of Emilie as usual. Raphaëlle phoned on the Saturday, a day after she'd left, saying she'd not be returning to Geneva for a while. She said she'd written to you in Montreal and asked if I'd stay on with Emilie until you arrived.' She paused. 'You've arrived.'

She rose and fetched an envelope from the mantelpiece, handing it to him. 'From Raphaëlle,' she said. 'For you.' She turned away and stared through the window. 'I don't understand why she wanted you to come back, I must confess. I always take care of Emilie whenever she's away.' Her spine was straight, her face full of a wiry, concentrated strength, the strength that brought her out of Russia in the late fifties and kept her travelling with a small child, Raphaëlle, first to Prague, then to Geneva where she began a new life. It was the same indefatigable stamina that enabled her to provide for Raphaëlle and raise her to be like her, sovereign and singular. Jack had always admired her for that, in spite of the hostility between them.

He rubbed his eyebrows as he watched Belle-Mère with her back to him. He wondered if she was withholding something. Why would Raphaëlle have gone off without telling her own mother or daughter where she was going? And Belle-Mère had a point – why would she invite him back to take charge of Emilie in her place? It didn't add up. But Jack knew Belle-Mère well enough to know she'd said all she wanted to for now.

Belle-Mère took out a blanket from behind the fold-down sofa, bade Jack goodnight and went to her room. Soon there was no sound at all in the salon but the guttering rain outside. Jack ached for a drink. He felt for the letter in his pocket, but wasn't up to reading it just yet. The very touch of the envelope made his heart race. He'd have to calm down a little. He walked over to the aquarium on the side table and watched two small coloured fish swimming to and fro between a line of air bubbles issuing from a ventilator tube. Raphaëlle's fish – she'd always loved fish. He gazed at their undulating fins as they propelled themselves effortlessly, soundlessly, patiently, from one side of the glass container to the other. Then, as if taking a cue from these tiny water creatures, he began pacing up and down the room. He paused after a while at the spot by the window where Belle-Mère had stood, and looked out into the night, hoping to see if the garden had changed. He brought his face up to the pane and peered towards the left of the veranda where he'd planted two trees for Raphaëlle after their wedding – a cherry and a Kilmarnock willow, both grown from seeds he'd brought from Ireland. *Prunus kuriliensis* and *Salix caprea pendula*. The names slipped unbidden into his mind. The willow was Raphaëlle's favourite with its small umbrella dome of bright green leaves, stiff weepy branches and pussy-willow flowers that blossomed for several weeks during early spring before the foliage emerged. He wondered if the foliage had come yet; if spring was early or late this year. But the trees slipped through the fingers of the dark. He'd have to wait till morning.

Still, he wouldn't wait to see Emilie. He removed his shoes and stole noiselessly into her bedroom. The bedside lamp was on, giving off a faint light through a lampshade covered on top by a Tintin book. A shock of curls peeped from the sheets covering her face. He moved up to the bed and stared at her, not breathing until he could hear her breathe.

There was enough light for him to recognise her features, her russet-brown hair, her strong mouth and freckles and the small indentations on the tips of her ears. He stared for several minutes, taking in everything about her hair and skin and breathing, struck by how much she'd changed in five years, how much more like Raphaëlle she'd grown. He placed his hand lightly on her head, careful not to wake her, like a monk administering a blessing. His fingers touched something metallic in her hair: she was wearing earphones. He removed them gently, a faint tinkle of music escaping into the warm air of the room before he switched off the Walkman beside her pillow and left, closing the door behind him.

5

Back in the living room, Jack took off his jacket and sat on the sofa. He opened the envelope Raphaëlle had left for him and removed the letter. He was ready now; but he still found himself hesitating. He slipped a cigarette from one of his duty-free packs and tapped it on the low coffee table, moving a small ceramic pot of red azaleas to one side. He held the cigarette between his fingers, but didn't light it. His breathing was fitful. Then he put the unlit cigarette back in the pack, unfolded the letter and began to read.

Dear Jack,

I'm leaving this note for you with Mother. She will stay on for as long as you need her and will tell you all you need to know – Emilie's school times, piano lessons, swimming classes, meal schedules, cleaning arrangements, shopping lists. There's no point asking Mother where I've gone, she doesn't know.

You're wondering, of course, why I asked you to come back and take care of Emilie like this, after all this time and all that's happened. I can't say right now, but trust me as I'm trusting you. Just as we did when we were close, when we lived in Cork that first year and everything was right between us. When we didn't even have to speak to know what was going on inside each other. When we spent hours every Saturday walking through the Gouganebarra forests as you named aloud the different trees, and we went to the cinema twice or more a week during those winter months – the Lee, the Ritz, the Pavilion, the Palace, the Capital, the Savoy, the Coliseum (I know more cinemas in Cork than in Geneva) – and went diving in summer in Lough Hine and sometimes off the pier at Currabinny. That deep, still, see-through water. Remember?

I recall each thing we did that year just as I try to forget so much of what has happened since. When things changed between us. At first I thought it was Sam's drowning, then Anselm maiming your leg with his car (I was never sure it was an accident). Then I thought it was the shock of learning I was pregnant and your arriving out here in Geneva, your leg in a strap, unable to find a job at first, unable to cope with me lying on my back for most of the day in a tiny apartment, six months pregnant; and even less able to cope when Emilie arrived.

But the real reason was your suspicion about me and Sam, wasn't it? No matter how often I told you Emilie was yours, you never believed me. When you read of Sam's desire for me in his diary, you couldn't help imagining we'd betrayed you. That was the moment doubt entered your soul. What you lost that terrible autumn of '77 was not just Sam, not just your leg – it was trust. That was the real maiming.

And that's when I first lost you. Not that we didn't have our good times, Jack, during our five years together in Geneva, sometimes lasting weeks, sometimes months; I know we did. Times when I almost believed that everything could be saved, that our life together really meant something. When we'd play the piano and laugh, or take Emilie up to the hills on our backs, or do funny poses for the camera and develop them in different size prints in the darkroom straight after, or lie in bed after making love and talk on and on about what we were thinking or reading or imagining, into the early hours of the morning. Times when you vowed you'd stay off coke for good and take extra classes teaching English to science students at *the city university and renew your plans to do a thesis on J.J. Toland. But after each good time the bad times just got worse, didn't they? You'd fall back to drinking again, and drugs, and miss classes and stay away for days on end and have me worried sick, each time more than the time before, until the night of the last overdose and Emilie's hysteria.*

So why call you back? I'm convinced that Emilie now needs to know her father – and I trust, from your letters (I read them all even if I didn't often reply), that you're not doing cocaine any more, that you're finally managing to come to terms with your addictions. There are other reasons too I can't go into now. Something extraordinary has happened that has changed my life.

Please be patient, Jack. I need time. Look after Emilie.

Raphaëlle

Jack folded the thin blue letter and put it back in its envelope. No mention of a man. No mention of her whereabouts. No clues whatsoever. Leaning forward on the edge of the sofa, he took his head between his hands and, to his surprise, this time an image of Raphaëlle did return, bit by bit, first the profile then the features, full and alive, emerging into vision like a photograph forming in solution. There she was waiting for him in Arrivals at Geneva airport when he first returned to her after his accident, eleven years ago, with her slanted cap and hazel eyes and hair the colour of dark honey and a crêpe-de-chine dress revealing the outline of pregnancy. There she was asking him how his leg was after the journey and telling him that she was feeling much better and had just got the promise of a job freelancing for a magazine in the city; then slipping a camera from her shoulder and getting some passenger in Arrivals to take a shot of the two of them. She with a hand on her crescent tummy, he with a crutch held high, both laughing.

Jack wondered what had happened to that photo. He could see it so clearly in his mind's eye. Raphaëlle's face, flushed and happy. Then his mind emptied again and light faded as he sank, little by little, into the night.

6

'Papa'.

Jack opened his eyes to see a pair of small, green-stockinged feet.

'C'est toi mon père?' The voice came from above, less whispered this time.

Jack rolled on to his back and gazed up into a freckled face. A head cocked sideways, eyes wide beneath long chestnut hair cut into a fringe in front. Dressed for school and smelling of toothpaste, she stood over him as he lay on the sofa. She didn't hold out her hand. She didn't bend to kiss him.

'Emilie,' said Jack. He raised himself on to an elbow.

'Tu te souviens de moi?' She wore a brace on her upper teeth which made her lisp slightly.

'Of course I remember you,' he replied in English. He'd always spoken in English with her as a child.

'J'ai beaucoup changée?' Emilie continued to speak in French.

'You're twice as big.'

'C'est normal, je suis deux fois plus âgée.'

'And you? You recognise me?'

'Oui. Mais tu es plus gros qu'avant. Dans les photos tu étais beau.'

'Thanks.' Jack smiled and stretched out his palm so Emilie could help him sit up. She didn't smile. She hesitated for a moment before complying. Her hand seemed so frail in his. The shock of its lightness made the back of his nose sting.

'I've come back to look after you,' he said, sitting upright. He felt as if he'd slept for days, right there on the sofa now bathed in strips of sunlight.

'*Je sais. Jusqu'à ce que Maman revienne.*'

'Soon?' He continued in English.

'*Bien sûr.*' She continued, matter-of-fact, lips pursed.

'Do you know where she's gone?'

'*Non.*' She looked towards the corridor and changed the subject. '*Tu as été dans sa chambre?*'

'I slept here on the couch last night.'

'*C'est bien. Maman n'aime pas qu'on fouille dans ses affaires. C'est là qu'elle travaille. Elle a ses choses à elle.*'

'I won't go into her room.'

'*Jure-le.*'

'I swear.' Jack gave a small laugh that sounded like a cough.

Emilie didn't laugh. She made a frown. '*Pourquoi tu es parti?*'

'It's a long story.'

'*Maintenant c'est Maman qui est partie.*' She looked away from him, then back again. '*Mais elle a ses raisons.*'

'But you don't know where she is?'

'*Non. Et Monsieur Defay ne sait pas non plus.*'

'The publisher?' Jack rubbed the puffy skin beneath his eyes then arched them wide.

'*Oui. Et il ne faut pas lui demander.*'

'Why not?'

'*Parce que.*'

'Because what?'

'*Parce que Maman l'a dit.*'

She left him sitting there and went to the table by the kitchen hatch. She poured cereal and milk into a pottery bowl. She ate with her earphones on, not saying another word but nodding her head to the music and mouthing words silently to herself between swallows. Jack asked what she was listening to when she removed the earphones to change her tape. 'Bullet the Blue Sky,' she replied, replacing the earphones. Her only words to him in English.

'Oh,' said Jack.

When she'd finished her cereal, she prepared a cup of coffee and took it to Belle-Mère's room. Jack wasn't asked if he wanted one. She fed the fish in the aquarium, a few sprinkles of red powder, then left for school. Jack said goodbye. She didn't.

He slumped back on the sofa and watched the door click shut. He put a hand to his throat. She was angry. He couldn't blame her.

7

Vous êtes bien chez Raphaëlle Feher-Feldring. Je ne suis pas là. Vous pouvez laisser un message après le signal sonore.

A shadow crossed Jack's heart. It was Raphaëlle's voice on the answering machine. Agile, sing-song, sure. He pressed 'pause' and moved to the other end of the bedroom they'd shared for five years of their lives.

He knew he shouldn't be here. He was alone. Belle-Mère was out for the day, Emilie at school. He lay on Raphaëlle's bed, face down into the pillow. The scent of walnut – or maybe it was jasmine – triggered carnal memories, seeping up like waters from a sunk well. Raphaëlle's neck and hair. Her far-away eyes, her stretched shoulders and breasts. Hands cupped open on the pillow behind her head. Her breathing coming in gasps. As in childbirth.

Jack was trespassing, invading Raphaëlle's privacy in ways she couldn't prevent. He turned on his back and reached over to a framed collage of snaps of Emilie at different ages, mounted on the wall above the bedside table. Emilie wearing a hat too big for her, Emilie painting a picture, Emilie swimming, Emilie blowing at a cake, Emilie at school. He replaced the frame and took some books from a small bookshelf behind the table. Dickens's *Tale of Two Cities*. Carter's *Wise Children*. Melville's *Moby Dick*. He was surprised. Raphaëlle rarely read anything but French and never liked Dickens. Maybe she'd been reading to Emilie at bedtime to help her English? He picked up *Moby Dick* and leafed through it. He stopped at a passage that Raphaëlle had ringed in blue ink, about a castaway called Pip: '. . . carried down alive to wondrous depths, where strange shapes of the unwarped primal world glided to and fro before his passive eyes . . . Pip saw the multitudinous, God-omnipresent, coral insects, that out of the firmament of waters heaved the colossal orbs. He saw God's foot upon the treadle of the loom, and spoke it; and therefore his shipmates called him mad.' He closed the novel briskly and put it pack on Raphaëlle's shelf. The back of his head smarted and he almost sneezed. He thought of Sam's drowning. He thought of Toland's God-of-matter. He thought of Raphaëlle's coloured fish. He thought of all of these things until he didn't know what to think.

In front of the bookshelf stood a bubble-glass vase of fading dahlias and laurel flowers, interspersed with bright-leaved orange blossoms – Raphaëlle had always loved the flowers of the South – and beside that, her miniature prayer book. He ran his fingers over the embossed ivory cover of the Hebrew Psalms given to Raphaëlle as a tiny child by her grand aunts before she left Odessa. The names of her mother's sisters, both prematurely deceased, were inscribed in hairline ink on the frontispiece – *Martha, Alicia*. Curious how it had belonged to both of them, he thought, the same thought he'd had the very first time he saw the inscription when Raphaëlle read from the book on their wedding day. Psalm 139, 10 April, 1978, Geneva.

He raised the prayer book and smelled it; he'd become quite an expert over the years at distinguishing different book odours, rather like the Eskimos being able to distinguish between different kinds of snow quite indiscernible to non-arctic dwellers. This one smelled of cherry with just the slightest hint of chestnut. He turned the thin frayed pages, his eyes washing over the filigree Hebrew letters that withheld their meaning from him. He understood the sacredness, but not the words. Hers not his.

He rose from the bed and returned to Raphaëlle's mahogany desk, catching a glimpse of himself in the wardrobe mirror as he passed. Still that wasted, post-inebriate look. His eyes hurt. He rubbed them and recalled how Raphaëlle used to stand before that same glass smoothing her eyebrows with her forefingers. He missed her. He'd always missed her. Since the day he lost her and every day since.

He opened his eyes and released the 'pause' button on the answering machine, its light still flashing. There were five messages. A young girl called Juliette asking Emilie to ring back. A dental receptionist rescheduling an appointment Raphaëlle had missed. Jean-Pierre Defay, Raphaëlle's publisher, confirming the rendezvous with Raphaëlle that last weekend in Yvoire. A woman called Pema, voice low and calm, asking Raphaëlle to return her call between eight and nine. And last, a man who didn't identify himself saying, 'I've sent the letter for you. *Bon voyage*,' followed by a piece of music. Jack played it back twice. It was definitely an overture with its wild and precise motifs, recurring and eliding, crescendo after diminuendo, but he couldn't put a name to it.

Who was this man with the music? And who was Pema? Perhaps Defay would know something. He was evidently the last person to see Raphaëlle before she went away. He'd pay him a visit.

He opened the cabinet door to the left of the desk to see if Raphaëlle's makeshift darkroom might reveal anything. It didn't. Just a cramped space full of clutter – half-empty bottles of chemical fixer in plastic trays, bits of a tripod, glass photographic plates, light metres, a zoom lens, rolled celluloid strips and underexposed contact plates, his father's old Leika. Raphaëlle had always done her professional work in a down-town photography bureau. This was just for domestic use.

Closing the door, he looked about him at the white walls. There was something chaste about them, minimal and meticulous. Raphaëlle had often said she wanted to live in a monk's cell; and Jack had always added – with lots of monks in it! – though Raphaëlle never found that very funny. The only images on any of the walls now were two lines of photo prints running from left to right over Raphaëlle's desk. All black-and-white and carefully hung like a row of frameless icons.

The first was a series of blow-ups of a black spot on a white background. The spot varied slightly in size and shape from photo to photo – pupil of an eye, aperture of an ear, vortex of a navel, void of an orifice, slit of a mouth, cleft of a sex. But each variation of the small formless chasm gaped out from the white celluloid surface as if summoning the onlooker to enter, to pass through the shifting rent at the centre of the image, traverse the gap between inside and outside, the cut where whiteness folded in upon itself or folded out on to matter – it was impossible to tell.

He took a step back to get a better look and squinted. He remembered the old riddle he'd heard at school once, the one that the Queen of Sheba put to Solomon about the room with ten doors: when one is open, nine are shut; when nine are open, one is shut. Answer: the ten doors are the human orifices; when the navel is open in the womb the other nine are closed; when the navel is closed up at birth, the other nine are open. Maybe Raphaëlle had been reading her Book of Kings. Maybe she'd taken to puzzling over the black hole hypothesis so dear to his McGill students. Or maybe she was thinking of nothing. Literally nothing. But it was never that simple, was it? After all, a hole is nothing – but you can break a leg in it. Jack knew something about that.

He tilted his head to see if a lateral view might reveal more. It didn't. He looked down at Raphaëlle's desk for a moment, absent-mindedly rearranging assorted bits and pieces, before raising his eyes again to inspect the second row of photo prints lining the wall beneath the black spot series. An extended seriograph of Saturn in multiple guises: chased by his castrating father, Zeus; beggared and naked on a crutch, genitals covered by a star; riding high in the cosmos over destitute children; leading a peasant revolt on horseback armed with scythe and sickle. Then Dürer's *Melencolia I*, Raphaëlle's favourite. A stooped figure with darkened face, head on hand, eyes vacant, wings taut on sloping shoulders, a bunch of keys suspended from the waist, compass in hand; above her head a tiny bell, hour-glass and scales; about her feet a scattering of squares, planes, nails and saws; and by her side, not just a sleeping dog, but – yes, Raphaëlle had always loved that touch – a cheeky angel perched upon a wheel, playing at nothing, creating from nothing. La Dame Mélancolie contemplating the waning of time against an ebbing tide. This was the engraving that got Raphaëlle going, set her off on her first illustrations for her first book. Jack wondered what she'd been after as he gazed upon this gallery of demon images. Soul-fear, black bile, *atris bilis,* angst, dread, *néant,* absence of being. So many names for the same thing. The same terrifying thing that choked his soul and hers after Sam's death.

A terrible tiredness came over him. He looked at his watch, on Montreal time – five in the morning. He'd hardly slept more than a few hours in the last two days. He didn't know day from night. He ached for some grass, but he didn't have any. Removing his shoes, he walked back to Raphaëlle's bed and lay down on the covers.

8

Jack woke after an hour, his back covered in sweat. He'd had another dream, the old recurring one he hadn't had for several years, the one he'd prayed he'd never have again: Raphaëlle having sex with a faceless, featureless man who took her in strange, forbidden ways and then stood back and reached a long arm back behind his head and pulled a zip from the base of his neck right over his crown and down his front until the skin fell away on either side and another man stepped out and walked back towards Raphaëlle lying there on the bed and kissed her and she kissed him back and the man was Sam.

He sat up straight and ran his hands over his moist face, shaking his head several times to make sure he wouldn't go back to sleep. He'd always hated this nightmare and what he hated most was that it wasn't just a nightmare – it was an erotic nightmare. That was what really frightened him, assaulted him like a hot-cold blast blowing up from a dark cavity within. Did he desire the very thing he feared – betrayal? Brother-betrayal, wife-betrayal, self-betrayal. What Raphaëlle called his *fantaisie du maquereau cocu*. His cuckold complex. Like the man in *Don Quixote* who drives his newly-wed into the arms of his best friend, then kills himself. Or the 'eternal husband' who entices his rival to his fiancée's house in order to arouse his desire, then triumph over it. Jack got mad every time Raphaëlle went on like that. But he'd always ask himself afterwards – was she right? Was his desire for her *through* his brother, *against* his brother, forever stolen *from* his brother?

Jack slipped off the bed and went over to the washbasin by the window, filling a glass with water and drinking it in one go. He returned to Raphaëlle's desk and resumed his search. Opening the top drawers, he located a number of black notebooks. He recognised them immediately. Raphaëlle's *journaux intimes*. Eleven in all, each with a year embossed in gold print on the spine. A green ribbon marked the last entry of the most recent one, dated 28 March 1989, the day before she left Geneva the previous week. He averted his gaze, but the pull was irresistible. Within seconds he was crouched over the open journal. The light was so dim he had to grasp the desk lamp by the neck and twist it down until the pages shone. The words were clear now, unmistakably hers. Each passage meticulously inscribed.

Days and nights in a big fish. Like Jonah in the belly of the whale. I sink where there's no foothold; I have come into deep waters and the flood sweeps over me. Formless matter. If I swim any further I will drown! So where can I go from here? Where can I escape? If I go, you are there; if I stay, you are here; if I just take off and settle at the furthest limits of the sea, even there you will find me, for you are part of me. Let's go by ourselves to some place, then, where we will be alone and rest for a time. Where we can taste a wisdom that sets free, guard each other like the pupil of the eye and start from where we are. At sea level. Let's find a lair and repose there. Arise then, my love, in the clefts of the rock, in the covert of the cliff, let me see your face, let me hear your voice; for your voice is sweet and your face is lovely.

He had no idea why Raphaëlle was suddenly so taken by

the Canticles. Some seemed familiar, but he couldn't place them. There was a tone of sweet sorrow about them. He leafed back through the previous days and weeks, certain he would find some hints as to the identity of Raphaëlle's 'love'. But there was nothing at all, not a single entry, between that last paragraph and early January – and then little more than short references to work assignments and rearrangements for holidays and some meaningless odd sentences. He closed the 1989 journal and sat back in her chair. He flexed his fingers at the joints, then started moving things about on the desk, exchanging the places of pens and pencils, fiddling with a box of paper-clips. His neck ached as if he'd pulled a muscle. He stroked it several times with his hand but it did no good; the pain got worse. He closed his eyes and remembered the way Raphaëlle would stand behind him and run her hands over his shoulders, loosening the knotted muscles whenever his panic attacks brought on bouts of fibrositis. And he also recalled the way she'd rub an imaginary mark on the base of her own palm as she spoke to him of things that flared inside her. The dark hurt of her eyes intensifying, her brows drawn together in a pleat, as her arms went out around his when he returned after one of his unexplained absences. And the way she'd cling to him some nights with wild awkwardness, her body temperature rising, tangles of loose hair moist from lovemaking streaking her forehead. At such moments her face would concentrate in a stare of distraction as desire grew unappeasable, her whole being tugged inward by some impossible demand.

He turned back and arched over the desk. He began leafing through some of the early journals, starting with one of the very first entries: the day Emilie was brought home from hospital.

3 May 1978. Came home with Emilie this morning at 10 a.m., three days old. Jack was waiting to meet us. A

bandage on his stitched leg now to go with his crutches. If this goes on, I told him, there won't be much left of him. I folded back a blanket and showed him Emilie asleep in my arms. Jack looked at her quickly and said she was just like me. He then started trying to explain what had got into him to go off drinking like that and overdose on drugs on the eve of Emilie's birth. But I told him now was not the time, that I was worried to death when he didn't turn up at the maternity ward and was almost relieved when I learned, the day of the birth, that he was recovering in the Clinique Générale. I guessed it was his old fear about Sam and me. Jack could hardly look at me, he just kept repeating how sorry he was, how unworthy he was to be with me, to be Emilie's father. Until I put my finger to his lips and said it was all right, to stop talking loudly like that or he'd wake Emilie. I gave him Emilie to hold and he took her. He spent hours examining her tiny long-nailed hands, her thousand-wrinkled feet, her long lashes and bottle-green eyes, repeating how like mine they were, and singing a song to her in a hushed voice, the same Irish nursery song over and over, until even I couldn't get it out of my head – 'You shall have a fishy on your little dishy/ You shall have a fishy when the boat comes home/ You shall have an apple, you shall have a plum/ You shall have a pear, when the boat comes home.' I thank God for this day and hope it's the end of Jack's doubt, the beginning of a new life for the three of us.

Jack lit a cigarette and brought the smoke deep into his lungs. His hands were shaking slightly as he turned the pages of the early journals back and forth, reliving each entry through Raphaëlle's eyes – the countless lapses followed by reconciliations followed by more relapses, promises and resolutions collapsing into new betrayals and lies, the addiction patterns becoming more and more predictable, compulsive, ineluctable, as his doubts drove him deeper into the mire of self-destruction and he would disappear for nights on end.

The entries that pained him the most, though, were not the descriptions of the bitter times, the details of recrimination and hurt – though these were painful too. No, the hardest entries for him to read now were the ones, scattered throughout Raphaëlle's diaries of their five years together, where she *believed*. Those moments when she convinced herself it had all come right again at last, for good, for ever, when she was persuaded Jack would really keep his word this time, when, in spite of all past evidence, *she still had faith in him*. Especially the time he was there for her in the winter of 1980 when her first major assignment was dropped at the last minute from the Geneva edition of *Arts et Métiers* – the piece on 'Masters of Melancholia: Homer-Dürer' – which she'd worked on tirelessly for almost a year. The first she knew about its omission was when she opened the December issue and found she wasn't in it. The editor hadn't even informed her of the magazine committee's decision. She wept for hours, sitting there on the sofa as Jack held her tight in his arms, a great deep silence between them, until she was calm and they ate a meal that Jack cooked and afterwards made love and he recited his favourite poem in Irish about the sea whispering love to the sand in a bay in an Aran island – *Cois cósta ag Cill Rónáin/ Chuala mé glór tomhaiste na bóchna/ Ag mórtas as a comhacht./ Ar na tránna beaga idir na carraigeacha/ Chuala mé an t-uisce ag siosarnach/ Foain ngrá leis an ngaineamh.*

He remembered that day so well, and the days after when he managed to rebuild Raphaëlle's confidence and encouraged her to take her work to a proper publisher and develop it into a book, which she eventually did, signing a contract with Defay just four months later. By the time they were ready to celebrate, however, he'd relapsed.

He turned to the fifth journal then and opened it at

the date of his final overdose. But there was nothing. Nothing about Raphaëlle's reaction on finding him lying unconscious on the floor, nothing about Emilie's hysteria and sedation and counselling. Nothing either about the bitter aftermath and her decision to split with Jack and his departure for Montreal. Just one blank page after another – until 10 October of that year, almost one month after she had asked him to leave. Her birthday.

Emilie and I went into town to celebrate my birthday. We had lunch at the Le Clos Vitré. She was all excited and kept asking about Jack. After a while, she began to mention the awful night. She doesn't remember much – Dr Kisiel says that's normal after hysteria attacks. I tried as best I could to explain about Jack's sickness, how his addictions sometimes led to blackouts like that. How it had started after his twin brother drowned, her Uncle Sam who was gone from this world before she came into it, but was like a part of Jack himself, they were so close. And I told her too about Jack losing the use of his leg just months later, and how the shock of both had filled him with such pain he did hurtful things to himself and to those he loved. I don't think she took much in – what can a five-year-old grasp of such things? – but she did say she never wanted to see him 'dead' like that again. It frightened her too much. She never wanted him to baby-sit again, she said. Then, seconds later, she was asking when Jack was coming back from Canada. In spite of everything she's terribly attached to him. It was the first time she had asked about him since he left, almost six weeks now. I said I didn't know, but that we'd say a prayer together tonight that he'd find peace in Montreal. She seemed content with that and finished what was left of her monkfish before ordering an adult helping of *tarte tatin*.

Putting her to bed tonight (she insisted on sleeping in

mine), Emilie reminded me about the prayer for Jack in Canada, then asked me to read *L'Oiseau Bleu* from start to finish, just this once, since it was my birthday. She fell asleep before I got to the end.

Now that I find myself trying to work here at my desk, I keep thinking of Jack. I have his first two letters open in front of me. I miss him so much, it's like a terrible ache inside me, a massive awful emptiness. But I musn't give in. Not this time. I mustn't respond. I must be strong whatever happens. I just can't allow it to happen again, as it always happened in the past. For Emilie's sake. For all our sakes. It's almost one in the morning but images of Jack keep coming back, like crisp flowers breaking open in the back of my mind. Especially the image of him lying there on the beach in Les Landes last May, slowly regaining consciousness, as I knelt beside him.

Jack leafed back though the entries until he came to May. He knew exactly where to find it: 23 May 1983, Les Landes, France.

9 a.m. The long drive down fom Geneva to Bayonne was unbearable. Jack and I rowed just before leaving the apartment when I discovered he had hidden stuff in his case. Emilie sang to herself in the back seat most of the way, looking out of the window and trying not to notice that anything was wrong. Seven hours of tension and heat. Last night, shortly after we arrived at the *camping*, we walked to a *méchoui* at Messanges and watched some Basque locals dance late into the night. They kept their hands and heads straight as their legs went crazy beneath them, hoisted up in all directions, their coloured trousers and smocks blazing beneath their half-coats. Like Irish dancers, Jack said. 'Dead from the legs up.' There was anger in his voice, standing there in the cool night surrounded by noisy villagers and tourists.

We slept well, though. Jack woke early and has gone for a walk on the beach. Emilie has made friends already with an English girl in the caravan beside us who invited her for breakfast. I need a swim to clear my head.

12 a.m. My God, Jack almost drowned! I met up with him on the beach as I was changing for my swim and asked him to join me. He didn't want to at first, but he came. We were scarcely out of our depth, twelve metres or so from shore, when huge Atlantic rollers took us in their undertow, twisting us down so fiercely neither of us could surface again, clamped to the sandy bottom by the monstrous weight above us. I tried bringing up my legs and knees, bucking desperately backwards and forwards against the gravity of the vortex, but I couldn't break the downward pull. I could no longer see Jack beside me in the churning current but knew it must be worse for him. I was out of breath and began to panic, sure we would both drown there, fastened to the floor of this cold sea, leaving Emilie behind us. And I instantly knew what Sam must have felt when he drowned off the rocks in Poul Gorm. I reached out instinctively, blindly, and found Jack's arm, his elbow, his hand, and pulled, and pulled again, until we rose to the surface. And as we floated up towards the air, I suddenly had an unspeakable thought. What if I let go? What if I let Jack float away like that, half conscious in the waves? What if he went the way Sam went? But I didn't let go. My hand clung to his until I dragged him to shore and pumped his lungs and kissed him back to life.

Jack knew that wasn't the end of the episode, however. He flicked over the page and read the final entry for that trip, two days later, 25 May.

On our way back to Geneva today, the wheel of the

2CV came loose near Ste Hermine and we had to stay overnight. Jack headed straight for the local bar and drank for hours while Emilie and I explored the tiny village. It had seemed so lifeless, vacant, nondescript from the main road – a real Vendéen backwater – but when we actually got to the centre, wandering through a maze of little streets, we found a square of perfect repose: a circle of silver beeches lit by a streetlamp and surrounded by two schools on either side – L'École Maternelle Publique and L'École Privée de St Paul et Ste Marie. And at the heart of the circle – or was it a square? – a low font bubbling with water and above it a monument with names engraved. *Aux Enfants de Ste Hermine Morts pour la Patrie 1914–1918, 1938–1945*. Emilie and I sat for a long time reciting those names. I'd read each one aloud and Emilie would repeat it back to me and sometimes ask if it was a man's name or a woman's name – Desiré Louineau, Alcide Guerineau, Dominique Riffaud, Honorée Taupier, Claude Meunier, René Loizelet. Then we'd count the years between the dates of birth and death to see if it was a child or a grown-up. And I even took some paper from my shoulder bag and wrote those names and surnames down. I'll keep it here in my journal. It's now after midnight. Jack has still not returned. He probably won't now before breakfast. Emilie is beside me, asleep. I listen to her breathing and want to keep her safe for ever.

Jack closed the journal and put it back in Raphaëlle's drawer with the others, his body hunched in loss. He couldn't read any more. He had to find her. Defay was the last to see her. He must know where she was. He must find her and talk to her. He phoned Defay and arranged a rendezvous for early that afternoon at his house.

As he waited for a cab to take him to Defay's place in

• Richard Kearney

Yvoire, the overture on Raphaëlle's answering machine kept revolving through his mind, following his thoughts like the fluttering tail of a kite. Suddenly it came to him – Gounod's *Faust*.

9

Jean-Pierre Defay's house was majestic. Exceptionally so for a modest publisher of middle-brow art and media books. Old money. Genevan Protestant banking family. Inherited capital. In any case, a fine eighteenth-century estate with rooms of robust proportions fronting the lake at Yvoire. Jack had already made one visit there eight years earlier when Raphaëlle was negotiating her first contract.

Defay met him at the front door with a brisk handshake. Over their heads, the tail-end of a rainstorm raided an overcast sky. Defay was older than Jack had remembered him, more white-haired now, wearing perfectly pressed corduroys and an open shirt with a cravat. Uncommonly handsome, he had an urbane, unruffled air about him. He knew why Jack had come.

He removed his duffel coat and followed Defay through a hallway of unswerving geometry, recalling how entranced Raphaëlle had been during their first visit by its architectural splendour – the vaulted entrance hall and balustraded stairwell, the inlaid parquet floors and second-storey drawing rooms panelled with book casements up to the ceilings. Re-entering that world of antique opulence, he felt shabby and uncomfortable.

'You might like to have a copy of Raphaëlle's work,' Defay said, reaching for a beige canvas folder on his bureau.

Jack nodded, his hands jammed in his pockets. He ran his tongue along the corner of his mouth.

'Raphaëlle was on her final shoot.' Defay poured two brandies. 'She was quite driven these last months, *vous savez.*' He handed one of the brandies to Jack.

Jack hesitated a second. It had been almost twenty hours since his last drink. He knew he shouldn't but he took the wide glass between the extended fingers of his two hands as if it were a chalice.

'It doesn't surprise me,' he said. He raised the glass and swallowed. Scalding gold. The hit was immediate, heat rising inside him like a shooting sap. 'It was just the same with her first book. The one on Saturn. Raphaëlle hunted through every gallery in Geneva. I'll never forget. Strip-searching back-room catalogues, basement collections, library holdings. Anything she could lay her hands on. Etchings. Woodcuts. Engravings. Frescoes. Murals. Oils. Drawings. Sepia prints.' He laughed. 'It got so bad at one stage our rooms were wall to wall with prints of child-eating fathers, cripples, beggars, miserable dames and every other damn kind of incurable depressive.' He gave a dry cough and took another swallow, sensing the impropriety of speaking so casually about someone he'd not seen for five years.

Defay smiled and turned away with a distracted air.

This made Jack even more uneasy. Raising his brandy glass to his eyes, he stared at the liquid level as if the contemplation of that fine golden line could steady him. Like a slice of ocean horizon.

'What's Raphaëlle's new book about?' he asked after a moment. He loosened his tie and sat down on a Louis XI chair by the bureau.

'Gemini,' Defay replied. 'Portraits of Gemini.'

'Twins?' He set his glass down.

'Yes. Over the last six months Raphaëlle has worked on nothing else. She's managed to photograph hundreds of them.'

'Why twins?' Jack's voice faltered. He began to rub the knee of his dead leg with the palm of his hand.

Defay shrugged and folded his arms across his chest. 'Raphaëlle called to see me about eight months ago and announced the new proposal.' He lowered his voice a little. 'From that day on that's all she talked about. Doubles. Rivals. Split pairs. Counterfeits. She never stopped.'

'I had a twin who drowned.' Jack felt his face flush.

'Raphaëlle mentioned that.' Defay raised his eyebrows. 'You were close, I gather.'

Jack nodded. He bent his head and stared at the varnished floor. 'Yes, though there were things about Sam I never understood. Raphaëlle was one of the few to get through to him. He died when he was twenty.' Placing his brandy glass on the floor between his feet, he got up and, asking permission with a lift of his brow, took a cigarette from a silver box on Defay's desk. He inhaled hungrily. 'Do you think Raphaëlle's book had something to do with her going off like that?'

'I've no idea,' replied Defay. 'We only talked about work. She came to me with reproductions, not explanations. Every few weeks she'd bring new prints. Mainly classical images at first. Romulus and Remus, Prometheus and Epimetheus, Castor and Pollux. The obvious examples. Then biblical ones like Jacob and Esau, Cain and Abel. And, after that, more exotic, unusual samples. Mayan pictograms of hero twins. Hindu prints of Yama and Yami. Yoruban sketches of sky doubles. And a batch of figures from obscure tribes in Papua New Guinea and the sub-Sahara, ones I'd never heard of.'

He pointed to the portfolio lying on the kneehole desk. 'They're all there. Raphaëlle was unstoppable. I had to keep reminding her of costs.'

'Copyright?' asked Jack vacantly.

'No, production costs. Colour illustrations are prohibitive these days.'

Defay moved from the stained-wood mantel to the table, opening the canvas folder and spreading the pages wide on either side.

'This one in particular cost a small fortune.' He nodded at a picture of two figures on a painted ceramic vase. 'Amerindian twins, eighth century, found in Belize. Raphaëlle spent days in Frankfurt in early March reproducing these prints at a Latin American exhibition there. It wasn't easy. These cylindrical shapes, you see. She first had to shoot the pottery design in sections, like this. Then afterwards she pasted them together, getting this effect here.' He was like a field marshal, poring over maps between campaigns. 'But that still left an optical distortion. So she hired a roll-out camera to get these continuous images of the glyphic designs encircling the vase.'

'How did she manage it?' Jack leaned closer, recalling what a perfectionist she'd always been whenever she prepared a photo shoot, brushing her hair up from her forehead with two fingers as she studied her light metre and focused her lens.

'She placed the bowls on a turntable,' explained Defay, motioning Jack closer to the pages on the desk. 'Then she photographed them with ultra-light-sensitive film moving through the camera at the same speed of rotation. That way she got the perfect copy. Look. Ingenious, no?'

Jack took a long pull on his cigarette. 'Was that the last thing she did?' he asked.

'No. After Frankfurt she went straight to London to get this print here.' Defay turned the page gently. 'It took two days to get such a technically perfect separation. It's called *The Cholmondeley Ladies*. Painted around 1600, anonymous.'

Jack blew smoke out of the side of his mouth and gazed down at the startling illustration in front of him. Two ladies with starched butterfly collars of lace, ceremonially enthroned in bed, one beside the other, each holding a baby wrapped in red and gold damask in their arms. So statuesque in their similitude, they looked like a mixture of tomb sculpture and cartoon. In the lower right-hand corner of the painting, an inscription, scarcely legible: 'Two Ladies of the Cholmondeley Family, born the same day, married the same day, brought to bed the same day'.

'Do these images mean something?' he asked with a nervous smile.

'It's what you see that counts.' Defay's features shone. 'Obsessions can't be shared, Jack.'

'You don't think Raphaëlle was trying to work something out?'

'She might have been. She made a lot of trips out of town these last few months.'

'Do you know where?'

'St Gallen mainly, a town about three hours away. She was working with someone there on Gemini archetypes.'

'Do you know who?' Jack sat forward.

'I never enquired. It's not my business. For me, it's the final product that matters.' Defay replaced his glasses and, looking down at Raphaëlle's folio, ran his hand over the smooth pages in front of him. 'Quite something, no?' He gestured to Jack to do likewise.

'Can I keep this copy?' asked Jack.

'Yes.' Defay carefully joined the canvas bindings and passed the folder to him.

Jack rose to leave, then hesitated. 'I know Raphaëlle visited you before she went away.'

Defay nodded.

'Did she visit a lot?'

'I told you, every few weeks since September.' He motioned vaguely towards a filing cabinet at the other end of the room. 'Whenever she wanted to show me new contact sheets, check her expense budget, extend her contract. Practical things.'

He looked out of the bay window near his bureau, raising his shoulders slightly. His voice grew more formal, guarded. 'Perhaps she came more often recently. She was trying to finish her book, you know, by the end of this month.'

'Do you think she went to St Gallen after she left here?' Jack asked.

Defay pursed his mouth and shrugged. 'All I can tell you is that Raphaëlle received an important call while she was here for the weekend and left almost immediately, cutting short her stay. I was sorry she left – we had decisions to finalise on the visuals – but it was clearly an urgent matter.' It was obvious from his tone that he had said as much as he wanted to say.

Jack stubbed his cigarette out and moved to take his leave. Defay started to accompany him, but Jack insisted on finding his own way out, his irregular footsteps clapping over the varnished oak floors and the curving flight of stairs.

Out on the lawn, he paused for a moment in front of the lake. The air smelled of wet grass. Wind buffeted the tall firs tilting towards the water as the sun made a coy appearance, glazing the wet slabs of stone lining the water. Was Defay telling the truth, he wondered? Was there really nothing between him and Raphaëlle? Nothing but professional acquaintance? And what were these trips to St Gallen?

He gazed intently at the lake, the border separating it from the garden a little blurred after the brandy. How many times had Raphaëlle swum in this same stretch of water, during summer sojourns, weekend visits, daily excursions, evening trysts, diving beneath its gilded waves, holding her breath as the buck of her spreadeagled limbs propelled her forward, deeper down into the aqueous dark, perhaps thinking things she dared not think when her head was back above water? About him. About Sam. About someone else?

He breathed deeply, once, twice, then again, almost snatching his breath the third time. As if the air had gone out of his life.

10

In the taxi back to Geneva, Jack did not once look out of the window. Nor did he speak to the driver. Loose memories of Raphaëlle continued to dislodge from the silt-bed of the past, floating up in bits and pieces like fragments of deep-sea wreckage. The early morning cliff walks near Myrtleville when she first came to Ireland on a photo assignment for her Swiss magazine, halting every five minutes to adjust her wide-angle lens to take shots of gannets or kittiwakes as they thrashed the sky and gulls pierced their ears with their demented cries. And blasts of wind vaulted up from the rocks beneath, blowing her hair over her face, and he hugged her tight in his arms as if to stay her fall into the waves beneath. Their visit to Jack's parents in the chalet above Poul Gorm, when they announced their engagement and Mrs Toland kept covering her tears and Dr Toland, in the last throes of cancer, gave her his old Leika, Jack his blackthorn stick, and apologised for not offering them a feast of prawns as the plankton that year had disappeared from the sea floor off the Galley Head. The year before Sam drowned.

He opened his eyes as the taxi drove down a steep incline near the lake. Lac Léman at its calmest. A vast expanse of water, silent and jade. He took his packet of cigarettes from his pocket and looked at it before putting it back again. He touched his upper lip with the tip of his tongue. His mouth was dry. He longed for a whisky to loosen him up, to lose himself a bit, to stay the eddies of remembering.

He spread the portfolio open on his knees, glancing randomly at one print after another. His breathing tripped and faltered as he leafed through Raphaëlle's gallery of images.

Painted frescoes of sun-moon siblings, Apollo and Artemis, Shu and Tefnut. An Egyptian tomb mural of Isis and Nephthys, sister twins rescuing brother twins, Osiris and Set, from the underworld. A double earthenware cup, bright blue and gold, a talisman of twinship in the Dogon tradition. Painted Babylonian twin-lovers in the shape of silver fish – Atargatis and Ichthys. Wooden carvings of Yoruba siblings, Taiwo and Kehinde, with plumed helmets and lozenge-shaped foreheads. Pueblo Indian doubles stitched in tapestry with bodies striped in black and white, corn husks tied to their torsos, deer hooves fastened to their ankles. Two portraits of Perez and Zerah struggling to be first out of Tamar's womb – one a ceramic cameo relief, the other a coloured thirteenth-century illustration from the *Codex Vindobonensis*.

Each image drew him further into Raphaëlle's labyrinth of doubles, making his mind swirl and spin until one particular illustration fixed his attention – a print of a Flemish portrait on the second-last page of the folder. A fifteenth-century painting from the Hermitage in St Petersburg, artist unknown. Two elegant ladies in matching brocade garments faced each other in profile. Seated in opposite fauteuils, they bore a family resemblance. Were they relatives, cousins, sisters? On closer examination, they looked like twins, identical twins. No, closer still, the *same* person. Same flaring eyes and clenched hands. Same silver necklaces and high coiffures and ochre complexions; even a tiny mole reversed just above the lip. Consumed by enmity, envy, adoration, objection? Impossible to say. He wondered if he were seeing things. Hearing things. Two women whispering to each other.

He closed the folio and squared it on his knees. Then he saw something through the transparent cover he'd not noticed when he opened it. On the front page, under Raphaëlle's name and the title, *Double Images – First Draft*, he read a dedication in a small typeface.

To Pema Spielereine.
St Gallen, 6 January, 1989

This had to be the Pema on the answering machine. The person Raphaëlle visited in St Gallen?

As soon as he got back to the apartment, he went to Raphaëlle's room, took out her last journal from the top drawer of her desk and located one of the journal entries that had puzzled him. Just three cryptic lines.

Why did one stay and one leave? Would it have been different if we'd stayed together, soulmates for the rest of our lives? Would we have been more ourselves or less ourselves? Rivals or allies? Ask Pema.

Was Pema the 'she'?

5

Jack was sitting reading in the living room when Emilie returned from school. She nodded casually as she passed him and went straight to her bedroom. Belle-Mère offered tea but Jack declined. She made some for herself. When she came back from the kitchen with her tray, he said he'd like to talk.

'Are you sure Raphaëlle wasn't involved with Defay?' he asked her.

Belle-Mère settled herself in the lounge chair opposite, affronted by the brusqueness of the question. 'If she was,' she said tightly, 'it's for her to tell you.'

'And Pema?' said Jack. 'Who's Pema?'

Belle-Mère's mouth creased slightly. 'Who told you about Pema?'

'No one. But I know Raphaëlle's dedicating the new book to her – Defay gave me a draft copy; and I came across a message from her on the answering machine . . .'

'You listen to private messages?' Belle-Mère lifted her tea and sipped.

'I'll do whatever it takes to find my wife.'

'Your former wife.'

'I'm sure she's in St Gallen. Defay said she often went there these last months.'

'She doesn't want you to follow her; hasn't she made

that clear?' Belle-Mère pursed her lips, not quite a smile, not quite a grimace.

'Yes. But I can't sit around here waiting.' He turned to face her. 'She's with Pema, isn't she?'

'I've told you Jack. It's Raphaëlle's business.'

Jack raised his eyebrows. 'Raphaëlle goes off leaving our eleven-year-old child behind and you say it's none of my business?'

Belle-Mère's eyes narrowed, but she didn't respond.

'You must at least have a number for this Pema Spielereine?'

Still Belle-Mère said nothing.

Jack struggled to his feet. Looking about him, he hobbled towards an address book by the phone on the side table. His leg felt leaden, the drag beneath the hip snagging his step. He opened the book and found Pema's address and number. He picked up the receiver, and held it in the air for a moment before putting it down again. If he called and Raphaëlle was with Pema, she'd probably tell him not to come. Better to go unannounced. He'd turn up on the doorstep and see what happened. 'I'm going to St Gallen to find Raphaëlle,' he said to Belle-Mère.

'*Moi aussi!*' Emilie chimed in from the doorway. She had changed from her school clothes into a long blue pullover and jeans.

'You can't go, Emilie,' said Belle-Mère sharply. 'You have school.'

'*Je vais plus à l'école avant le retour de Maman!*' Her lips made a resolute pout.

'*Si,*' replied Belle-Mère.

'*Non!*' insisted Emilie. She turned to Jack. '*Papa? S'il-te-plaît, Papa?*'

Jack met his daughter's gaze, then turned to Belle-Mère. 'I'm going to St Gallen tomorrow and I'm taking Emilie with me.'

'You can't.' Belle-Mère stiffened and rose slowly to her feet.

'Pack whatever you'll need,' Jack said to Emilie.

Emilie nodded and went to her room. Belle-Mère followed her, not looking once at Jack.

12 $\int$

Jack decided to take a morning train the next day. St Gallen was one of Switzerland's oldest monastic towns, nestling between the Alps and the Bodensee, founded by an Irish monk in the seventh century. It was also the place where he and Sam had shared their last summer together with Raphaëlle, a coincidence that only added to his increasing puzzlement.

Emilie had made a scene in the hallway before they left for the station, saying that Raphaëlle always allowed her to bring her *poissons* along whenever they went on holiday. She produced a portable aquarium from one of the hall cupboards which she claimed was specially for travelling. Everybody brought their pets with them in trains these days, she explained, dogs and cats and mice and guinea-pigs in little baskets with litter trays and ventilation holes. But Jack replied firmly, 'No fish!' They were not on summer holidays now and the proper place for these little 'guppies' was here in the flat where Belle-Mère could feed them. They weren't guppies, Emilie snapped, pointing to the tiny fish in the aquarium on the hall table, they were exotic tropical creatures with elaborate sail-fins and wonderful rainbow colours. Jack said the answer was still no, and if they didn't hurry up they'd miss the train.

They made it just in time, finding seats at the back of

the train. Emilie, plugged into her Walkman, sat opposite Jack and refused to look at him for the first hour of the journey. After she'd changed her tape for the second time, she opened a shiny carrier bag and peered inside. She reached in and took out a selection of Tintin books, scrutinising each cover one after the other. *Tintin au Tibet. Le Lotus Bleu. Le Trésor de Rackham Le Rouge. Le Secret de la Licorne. Coke en Stock.*

'Why do you like Tintin?' asked Jack. 'There are no girls in it.'

'*Quoi?*' She wrinkled her nose and removed one of her earphones to hear him repeat his question.

'There are no girls in Tintin, are there?'

'*Et alors!*' She replaced the earphone, glaring at him with charcoal eyes. She went on reading, her little ears flattened back like an irate cat's. Jack watched. He couldn't get over the fact that she wore different clothes each time he saw her. Today she was wearing a pink T-shirt under a green cardigan of thick wool; and, around her waist, no doubt for the journey, a belt with a K-Way anorak wrapped in a polythene pouch. Jack wondered how a whole jacket could fit into such a tiny container. He also wondered how Emilie could manage to pack three full changes of clothes – along with other belongings – into a single knapsack.

He looked up at his own bag on the luggage rack above. He'd brought only one change, along with his wash things and a few Toland volumes. His immediate impulse was to reach up and take his notes from the bag, but he didn't. Almost two days now without a thought for his namesake; it was hard to credit. He glanced towards the window to see a dim reflection of his own face staring back at him. And behind his reflected face, another face, Emilie's, watching him watching himself. '*Tu ressembles à un perroquet chauve,*' she said.

Jack laughed flatly, then looked through the pane at the passing landscape. Savoy vineyards and woods rolled by, then the village of Carrouge stacked against the hillside with maroon-tiled roofs over shuttered windows; and he thought how many times Raphaëlle must have made this same journey. Montreal already seemed light years away, Danièle and his other colleagues like ghosts from a pre-existence. He was back in Raphaëlle's world now. Other things were tugging at his soul.

He wouldn't read Toland; he'd read Raphaëlle. He slid the folder Defay had given him from the carrier bag by his side and opened her collection of prints. It was his first chance to look at them properly since the taxi ride from Yvoire the previous day.

The opening section was a sequence of Gemini prints from Greek and Roman myth. Urn line drawings, woodcuts, frescoes. His eyes feasted on the curious creatures on the pages before him. Castor and Pollux, Prometheus and Epimetheus, Romulus and Remus. Then he turned to the commentary on the last page of the section, inscribed in Raphaëlle's exiguous but fluent longhand. The words were detached, impersonal, dispassionate, but to Jack they were passion itself.

COMMENTARY: *Greco-Roman tradition recounts several foundation myths of twins. Greek mythology tells of Epimetheus, who remained faithful to earth, and his twin Prometheus, who rose to the Olympian heavens and stole the secret knowledge* (gnosis) *which he then bestowed on humans, endowing them with creative power* (techne demiourgike). *As a result of Prometheus's theft, mortals acquired the art of speaking, building, farming and weaving, enabling them to forge society. Prometheus was punished, tied to a sacrificial rock where an eagle ate his liver.*

A later Greek story of inaugural twinning is the myth of the hermaphrodites. Fearing their pride, Zeus cut the original men-women in half. After this bi-section, the human race was made up of cloven selves wandering around in search of each other. Sexual desire was the longing to reintegrate one's former double, or in Plato's famous words, 'to make two into one, bridging the gulf between one human half and another'.

Castor and Polydeuces founded Troy. They were born from the wedding of Heaven and Earth. Zeus, in the form of a swan, ravished the mortal Leda who laid eggs from which two pairs of male-female Gemini emerged. From the first issued the mortal pair Castor and Clytemnestra; from the second, the immortal pair Polydeuces and Helen. While Castor was dark and anguished, Polydeuces shone with celestial brightness. Both fought to avenge the abduction of their sister Helen of Troy, but Castor, being mortal, was killed. So grief-stricken was Polydeuces at the death of his twin, he begged Zeus to let him die so that his brother might return to life. As a compromise, Zeus allowed them to trade their lives, living one day, dying the next. One remained in darkness while the other paraded the sky. At the close of day, they passed each other and changed places. For ancient Greeks the zodiacal sign of Gemini – in Greek Dioscuri – signalled the duality of humans as partly transient, partly divine. Hence the etymological connection between Gemini and genius. The glyph for Gemini – twin parallel columns of dark and light – refers to the Gates of Hercules (the solar twin of lunar Iphicles) which open on to the world of opposites.

Castor and Polydeuces (Pollux in Latin) are the most famous symbols of astral doubling. Identified as the morning star, Pollux was the first twin to rise, heralding the chariot of the sun and dissolving the first rays of light; while Castor's evening star remained visible to the last, accompanying the setting sun on its journey under the earth. Twilight – twinlight – thus came to denote the half-light of matinal and vesperal transitions to day and night. Castor and Pollux epitomise heads of twins in the constellation of Gemini.

Balancing each other in perfect symmetry, these stars are associated the world over with doubling. Identical at first regard, distinctions begin to emerge on closer inspection.

Astronomers have discovered that while Pollux is a huge orange star just 35 light years from Earth, Castor is comprised of two planets revolving about each other 45 light years away.

In Latin myth, Rome was founded by Romulus and Remus, born from the coupling of a king's maid with a disembodied phallus. Abandoned by the king, the twins were fostered by a wolf and eventually returned to the Tiber to build a city. Falling into dispute as to where to build their city, Remus was killed. Romulus buried his brother under the Palatine hill on which the eponymous city was constructed.

So what do these legends tell us? That twins are the same or different? Natural or unnatural? Born of one or born of two? Spawned by man, or God, or beast . . . ?

Jack gazed from the words in front of him back to the prints on the preceding pages. He feasted on the images, ravenous to extract whatever secrets they held about Raphaëlle, who had put them there. He scoured and scanned the exotic creatures, one after another, looking for hints and signs. The earth-sky twins, Epimetheus and Prometheus, slim-limbed, soft-boned, arms joined. The celestial Dioscuri changing places in the firmament. Romulus and Remus locked in mortal combat.

A memory loomed up from the distant past like bog-cotton through fog. Sam, stealing Jack's photo of the whale, the photo their father had given to Jack for being so brave, for not panicking like everyone else in the trawler that day when the whale had buffeted the keel with its dorsal fin, and Sam had run into the cabin and cried. The stolen photo, the first of many thefts. Jack could not look upon these prints of Gemini without thinking of Sam.

But what did Raphaëlle see as she hunted through these Gemini images? Which was Sam for her and which was he? Bright immortal Polydeuces or death-bound Castor? Victorious Romulus or vanquished Remus? Skyward

Prometheus or his earthy sibling? And why did Raphaëlle choose stories of twin-birth tied to trespass – Leda raped by a swan, the king's maid ravished by a disembodied phallus? Who did Raphaëlle see as trespasser?

Jack longed to voice these questions to Raphaëlle herself, to find her quickly wherever she was and talk to her and ask her once and for all what Sam had meant to her.

He looked across at Emilie lying back against her carriage seat now, eyes closed, a scatter of freckles across her cheekbones, her head rocking gently to the music from her earphones. Half asleep like that, Emilie looked so like Sam when he was a child – the same smooth pallid complexion, the same resolute mouth and chin. Old fears began to surge up inside Jack, like little blind bats swarming in a cave. He wished he was out in the open air. For too long he'd been pottering in others' minds and souls, snagged in games of splittling and splicing, desiring what others desired, losing himself in others' lives, posthumous lives, his brother's, his namesake's – until there was nothing of his own to live.

13

Jack put one hand to his throat. Above all, just now, he wanted to do right by Emilie. But he was having misgivings. Hardly halfway into the journey, and he was already wondering if he should have brought her along, allowing her to miss school like this. He'd made the decision on impulse, almost to spite Belle-Mère, or to prove something to Emilie. But worse, he wasn't even sure they'd find Raphaëlle with Pema when they reached St Gallen. And if they did, she might well be furious with him for following her like this and bringing Emilie along. She'd asked for time in her letter, after all. She was quite clear about it.

He swallowed hard. He was out of his depth and he knew it. He began to breathe rapidly and perspire about the neck. Initial symptoms of the panic-attack he knew too well. He looked up at the case on the overhead rack containing two half-litre bottles of duty-free Jameson he'd bought on the flight over. But he couldn't drink neat from a bottle in a carriage like this, not in front of Emilie; and he had no glass. He looked down at his hands in his lap for a moment. He curled his fingers and examined his nails. Then, pushing both palms down on the table, he heaved himself slowly to his feet.

'I'm going to the buffet carriage. Would you like something?' he asked.

'*Non*,' Emilie replied without looking up from her trinkets.

'No, thank you,' he corrected.

'*Non*,' she said again, distractedly, still not looking up.

14 ∫

When Jack returned to the carriage, fortified by a few quick shorts, Emilie had changed her mind. She'd like something after all, she said, removing her earphones. He told her what was on the buffet menu and she chose *coquille de poisson* and a glass of Orangina. Jack nodded, averting his face slightly to conceal the alcohol on his breath. He went back to the bar and returned a few minutes later with Emilie's food in a polythene-covered container and two orange juices one for Emilie, the other, spiked, for himself. Emilie ate while Jack sipped his drink and leant sideways against the window for a quick nap.

He was woken by Emilie poking at his shoulder as they passed the station before St Gallen. He yawned noiselessly and began to feel his absent leg again. He reached down and rubbed his knee. That funny feeling of not knowing where his lower half was, of one of his limbs not living, not being there, like paste or sand, part of his flesh but not his. Nulling, the doctor in Limerick had called it after his accident, when the neural traffic in his lower body ground to a halt. Nulling. The word came back to him like an old nickname.

He thought of trying to describe it to Emilie but realised it was too complex. He recalled how he'd once tried explaining it to Raphaëlle and how difficult it was. She'd asked if it was like the feeling of nerves being crushed after sleeping on a limb, and he'd said yes, in a way, but that such feelings were temporary, the half-numbness already announcing the return of sensation through the tingling of joints and synapses. Then Raphaëlle had described her feeling of spinal anaesthesia when giving birth to Emilie, a peculiar sensation of non-sensation in one whole part of her, an out-of-body experience while still in her body, strange uncanny, extra-terrestrial. But that was different, Jack had replied, as she was giving birth to another being, Emilie. Nulling gave birth to nothing.

He reclined in his seat and looked again at his daughter, who was utterly absorbed with a box of odds and ends splayed randomly across the Formica tabletop. Baubles, costume jewellery rings, coloured pens, mascara, hair bobs, charms, gems, and a string of shiny beads. Simple, basic, tangible things. She was breathing through her slightly opened mouth, her tongue moving over the brace on her upper teeth, as she replaced each item in the container. She cocked her head to one side just as she used to do when acting the clown for Raphaëlle when still a small child, her lips in a moue, her face in a funny pose, or when she perched herself beside her mother at the piano, pretending to rehearse Diabelli's Opus 149, Number 6, for four hands.

Jack stared at her chestnut curls pushed up above the earphones, her strong, handsome little face impervious to the world passing by outside the window, and to the crowded carriage inside, and to him, her father, watching her across the space dividing them.

He took another swig from his glass and wished the train would arrive.

PART III

She stared at the print of Christ and Thomas in front of her. It had taken her almost three days to get it right, to sort out permissions, secure the negatives, developing them first as contact plates, then into full-scale photo prints. Now it was ready. The image was hers. The Risen Christ with Thomas the Twin. Only the commentary remained. A few more paragraphs. She worked slowly, the way she always worked.

From the Fall of Adam to the coming of Christ, the Bible recounts many tales of twins – Cain and Abel, Isaac and Ishmael, Jacob and Esau. This last pair fought within their mother's womb but Esau was the first-born, with Jacob grabbing at his heels (Gen. 25). Esau, the 'red one', was hairy and strong, symbol of the sun's fire; Jacob, smooth and cunning, was white-skinned like the moon. Jacob stole his brother's birthright and was later struck in the thigh as he wrestled with an angel through the night. 'There wrestled a man with him until the breaking of the day' (Gen. 32). In this struggle with his demon, Jacob received the name of Israel. He saw God face to face.

The next twins in Genesis issued from incest: Tamar slept with her father-in-law Judah and gave birth to Perez and Zerah (Gen. 38). Judah carried the coveted blessing of his father Jacob, and so his sons competed for the privilege of 'first-born'. The sibling enmity began in Tamar's womb when the one who was to come out second came out first. He was named Perez, meaning breach, the one who supplanted his brother. While she was in labour, one put out a hand; and the midwife took and bound on his hand a crimson thread, saying: 'This one came out first.' But just then he drew back his hand, and out come his brother; and she said, 'What a

*breach you have made for yourself!' Therefore he was named
Perez. Afterward his brother came out with the crimson thread
on his hand; and he was named Zerah (Gen 38. 27–30). In
fact, the crafty Tamar married two of Judah's sons in addition
to sleeping with Judah and bearing him twins – whence the
famous riddle of the Queen of Sheba: 'A woman married
two and had two sons, but all four of them had one father.'
Answer: Tamar!*

*Gnostics believe it is no accident that Perez and Zerah are
cited on the very first page of the Gospel as the first direct
'ancestors' of Jesus Christ (Matthew I:1–6).*

*The biblical chain of twins culminates with Christ and
Thomas – Thomas Didymus, Thomas the Twin – the double
who dared Jesus to reveal himself, who wrote a Gospel revered
by Gnostics but censured and buried for two thousand years.*

She placed a piece of blotting paper over the page and
leaned back in her chair. She put her pen down and,
inhaling the odour of wood polish, ran her fingers along
the edge of the shiny oak table. The noise of the air-
conditioner behind her was like a whirr of wings. Resting
her chin on the apex of her joined hands, she gazed about
her at the row of terracotta busts with their unseeing faces
– Buffon, Peiresc, Gastelier, Condé, Richelieu, Mazarine.
Noble heads perched between Louis XVI chests and rose-
wood pendants and illuminated by bronze-framed lustres
of the seventeenth century. Then she turned in her chair
and looked out of the high latticed window. She gazed
long and earnestly, as if regarding her own reflection in
the glass, though she was not looking at herself at all, but
at the river, clear, glinting, opaline, passing by the row of
poplars outside. And as she stared she thought about the
black gash, the gap in God's side. What it might mean. If
Christ was the body of the cosmos, what was this hole in
the heart of the world? The vortex of matter? The nil point
around which all things turn, from which all things come,

and back to which all things return? The nothing out of which Yahweh created the world – *ex nihilo*?

She reached across the table for Augustine's *Confessions* and opened it at Book XII. Augustine's answer to the Gnostics: 'From nothing, then, you created heaven and earth, distinct from one another . . . invisible and without form the darkness reigned over the deeps . . . It was a great chasm over which there was no light . . . For even in its deepest parts the ocean which we can now see has its own kind of light, discernible to fish and the living creatures that crawl upon the sea-bed, but in those days the whole world was little more than nothing, because it was still entirely formless . . .' And as she read she thought of those Gnostics who fought with Augustine and wanted to make this formless matter part of God, the fallen part, the nether part, the shadow of his being. Those who said it was the pupil of his eye, the gaping mouth through which the First Word sprang, the breach in the Absolute from which all impurity and imperfection issued into our world. And thus they made of God a being extended through space to infinity, a being whose non-being was itself a part of him, for whom evil was part of his substance, only shorn, shed, doubled, exiled. Like a lost twin. That's why Augustine rose against the Gnostic God, the duplicitous God, the God of evil-good.

And she thought too of what the black gash meant to her. How it exposed itself when dark times came, when doubts swallowed her up as they swallowed Thomas the Twin. The crack in the window of her own mind, the stain on the glass of her soul, the rent where fantasms clustered and swarmed, like bees around the mouth of a hive.

She put a hand to her forehead, then closed the red leather volumes in front of her, one after another. She ranged them in a pile – a smell of mustiness and mildew wafting up from the worn bindings – and placed it beside the print of Christ and Thomas. Almost there, she said to herself, covering the print with a protective diaphanous sheet. Almost there. Another day or two and she'd be finished.

ST GALLEN

'How long will you turn your face away from me?'

Psalm 13

5

Jack and Emilie walked up Gallusstrasse from the station. The copper spire of the Klosterhof crowned the skyline as it had twelve years ago when Jack visited St Gallen with Raphaëlle and Sam. But he didn't want to think about that now; he had his daughter with him, and an address in his pocket. Pema Spielereine, 144 Jacob-Strasse.

They cut an odd figure, invalid father and earphoned daughter, as they made their way past St Laurenzkirche. As they turned on to the Marktgasse a flock of pigeons flared and veered away. Emilie hiked her shoulders back, spooked by the clatter of wings. Jack stepped forward and shooed the birds with a fanning motion of his stick. He then hoisted his blackthorn towards the irregular dormer roofs of blackish-red stone. Typical of the old town, he pointed out, like the aromas of fresh baking and coffee wafting from the cafés. Emilie said nothing but paused for a moment, looked up and inhaled.

In the middle of the Marktgasse, Emilie spotted a street entertainer and pulled Jack by the cuff. Dressed as a clown with a tall top hat, the man summoned a few passers-by into a small circle. Jack and Emilie joined them. The man said he'd show them the trick of doubling the number of a group in half a minute. On the count of three, the handful of people were to burst into a loud cheer. As instructed, at three, a prolonged roar rose into the air. And sure enough, just as he had promised, figures appeared from everywhere – street corners, kiosks, bus stops, cafés – piling into a large circle three or four deep. The new arrivals looked over the shoulders of the original onlookers, curious to see what had made them laugh. But the street clown had melted in with the group, leaving a gap at the heart of the circle. There was nothing to see. Just empty space.

Jack frowned as the bystanders dispersed, but Emilie laughed. They moved on then, past the square, until they came to Jacob-Strasse. He couldn't help scrutinising each woman passing in the street, as if he somehow expected Raphaëlle to appear – 'out of the blues'. They located number 144 but there was no reply. Jack knocked several times. Not a sound inside, except for a telephone ringing, once, twice, unanswered. They were about to turn away when they heard someone shuffle towards the door. A middle-aged woman answered, with arched brows and cornflower-blue eyes, bright and glossy as a doll's. She smelled of cooking.

'*Gruetzi,*' she greeted them in Schweizerdeutsch.

'Pema Spielereine'? asked Jack.

'*Nein,*' the woman replied. She spoke gently but formally.

'Is – she – here?' Jack emphasised each syllable.

'*Nein. Sie isch gange.*'

'Where?'

'*Ich weiss nid.*'

'Did a woman called Raphaëlle stay here?' persisted Jack.

'*Ich weiss nid. Ich weiss nid,*' and she shook her head back and forth like a lead pendulum.

Jack and the lady laboured through further monosyllabic exchanges until it became obvious that Frau Spielereine had recently moved without leaving a forwarding address. Their best chance, the woman suggested, was to try the Klosterhof where Frau Spielereine worked sometimes.

Someone there might know. He thanked the woman and moved off.

'*Ça sent mauvais chez elle*,' said Emilie as they made their way down Jacob-Strasse.

'We probably interrupted her at her cooking when we knocked,' offered Jack. He sniffed the air. 'Smelled like smoked herring to me. Maybe haddock.'

'*Pour son chat, j'espère*.' Emilie wrinkled her nose.

On their way up to the abbey, Jack recalled a Dr Klaus, director of the Klosterhof archives, whom they'd met during their last visit; he might be able to help them.

He lifted his head occasionally towards the sky. The clouds to the north were troubled with late snow, and to the east the high mountains, luminous white just a few minutes earlier, were beginning to shade into blue folds, marking out a ragged hem against the evening sky. He stepped carefully, hesitantly, along the pavement, like someone moving over hazardous ice, not sure just where he stood. What was he doing dragging his daughter along in search of Pema Spielereine, a woman he knew nothing about?

2

By the time they arrived at the Klosterhof, reception was closed. It was just past 7 p.m. Jack wanted to enquire if Dr Stavrogin Klaus still worked there but there was no one about. He rang the bell several times without response. He was moving off, cursing to himself, when Emilie caught sight of a string of announcements on the reception noticeboard. One bore the name of Pema Spielereine, instructor at the St Gallen Centre of the World Community of Christian Meditation. Seminars on 'Jung and Gnosticism', held on alternate weeks in the Klosterhof and the Müller Hotel. Telephone and fax number listed.

Jack scribbled the address of the hotel on to the back of his McGill library card. They found it without bother, just opposite the public entrance to the Stiftskirche, a modest, neo-baroque four-storey lodging. Jack asked the manager, Herr Müller, if a woman called Raphaëlle Toland was staying there. Müller said he'd never heard the name, then corrected himself, saying there was someone called Raphaëlle Feher-Feldring who often registered for the Spielereine seminars. Jack explained that she was his wife, going by her maiden name. Müller nodded, smiled and said she was a regular guest and always gave great attention to Margarita, their twelve-year-old daughter. She'd last visited the hotel, Müller said, two weeks ago, for the final weekend work group of the series; he hadn't seen her since. He gave Jack Pema Spielereine's new address and said she might know where Raphaëlle was.

Jack thanked him, left the bags at reception, and proceeded with Emilie into the hotel restaurant where the evening sitting was almost finished. Emilie was delighted with the hotel. This was, after all, where Raphaëlle had been staying when she phoned her from St Gallen during her weekends with Pema Spielereine. And it had a big aquarium in the reception hall with Black Pacu fish with glistening white scales and huge eyes all the way from the rivers of South America; and a phone and multi-channel TV in each room.

After a light supper of plaice and fried potatoes – Emilie ate everything on her plate and anything Jack didn't eat on his – they went up to their rooms. Jack installed Emilie in hers first, a modest single room, rose-coloured, with dark oak bedding chests and folksy carved dressers. Polished copperware hung from the walls and a bowl of bird's-foot violets adorned the bed table. Emilie immediately set to inspecting the violets, checking if they were real or plastic, then turned on the TV.

'Don't stay up too late,' said Jack. 'It's been a long day.'

Emilie emptied a pile of books, baubles, and clothes from her bag on to the bedspread. She said she'd probably watch TV for a bit before turning off the lights. Jack nodded, kissing her goodnight on the forehead before he left. She frowned.

3

Jack would have to wait but it wouldn't be long till morning. It was already after 10 p.m. He wondered what he'd do about Emilie. He couldn't take her to Pema Spielereine's house – he didn't know what he'd find – and he couldn't leave her alone in the hotel. How foolish he'd been to bring her to St Gallen! He dialled Herr Müller at reception, who said there'd be no problem leaving Emilie with Frau Müller while Jack went to his meeting in the morning. Emilie could play with their daughter Margarita when she got home from school at two.

Jack thanked him and put down the phone. This stroke of luck deserved a drink. He helped himself to a large one from his duty-free supply which he'd tucked away in the dresser, then lay on the bed and tried to sleep. But the whiskey made his mind spin and images of Raphaëlle tumbled back into his brain. He wondered if she'd slept in this same room, in this same bed, in these same sheets? He swung both legs to the floor and took Raphaëlle's folder from his bag. Sitting on the side of the bed, he opened it at the second section. A spread of graphics held his gaze. Blown-up scans of twin foetuses. From myth to medicine! He clicked his tongue against the roof of his mouth, baffled by Raphaëlle's interest in science.

The illustrations were divided into two columns. The left-hand one featured fraternal twins – chlorion and amnion: two hooded sperm mushrooming up like tiny atom bombs within the parallel light bulbs of the ova. The right-hand column showed identical twins – one egg and one sperm splitting to form a zygote. The graphics reminded Jack of the coloured pictures in his father's medical books in Sydney Parade which he and Sam had browsed through hundreds of times after primary school as they sat waiting for a lift home. Photos of retinas and irises, corneas and globes, cataracts and lenses, usually diseased, bloodshot or bloated. Especially the shots of glaucoma sufferers circled in red by their father, Dr Joseph Toland, glaucoma specialist, one of Cork's three eye surgeons, Joey Eyes for short. Only the images before Jack now were eggs, not eyes. Unseeing. Blind. Hidden. Almost obscene in their glabrous secrecy. Like mucous fungal growths in a minuscule hothouse. More vegetal than human.

He gazed upon them for some time before lighting a cigarette and serving himself another stiff drink. He drew hard, exhaling the white smoke through his nose. Then he turned to Raphaëlle's commentary at the end of the sequence, surprised by the moistness of his hands as they touched the paper.

Twins are conceived more often than they are born. Many foetuses do not survive the early stages of development. For every pair of twins who reach term, up to two other pairs are originally conceived (not surviving beyond the first three months of pregnancy). Approximately 1 in 80 births worldwide are twins.

Two-thirds of twins are dizygotic, that is, result from two eggs being fertilised by two sperm. These are called 'fraternal twins' and, genetically, are no more alike than other sisters and brothers. The other one-third are monozygotic or 'identical' twins, resulting from a single sperm fertilising a single egg which then divides into separate foetuses. These twins are same sex and share 100 per cent of their genes. In occasional pairs, identical twins may be opposite-handed and have moles on opposite cheeks or hair whorls on opposite sides of their scalps. These are known as mirror-image twins. One hypothesis to explain identical twinning is that there are impaired cells in the early-developing zygote, resulting in an attempt to shed the defective elements – the shed half then developing into the identical twin foetus.

In addition to dizygotic and monozygotic twins, a third possibility exists. So-called 'intermediate' twins can develop when the mother's egg divides prior to fertilisation and the two halves are fertilised by different sperm; or when two eggs from the same ovarian cycle are fertilised by different men (a rare but not unknown phenomenon called superfecundation*).*

Twin transfusion syndrome is due to one foetal twin receiving a more generous blood supply than the other. This results in the former being reddish in colour due to high haemoglobin levels of red blood cells, while the latter is pale because of anaemia.

The European rate for twin-births is about 10 per 1,000 (Ireland 11.6) in contrast to the Far East (average 5.6) and certain sub-Saharan African countries, such as Ghana and Nigeria, where the Yoruba tribe of 18 million people has an incidence rate of up to 60 per 1,000.

Remarkably little is known about the causes of twinning.

Jack closed Raphaëlle's folder and removed his shoes. Raising his feet on to the bed, he lay back on the pillow and stared up at a ceiling crack that spread out from the plaster frieze in a cluster of stray filigree lines. He tried to make out a figure but couldn't. Why was Raphaëlle so fascinated with birth-rates? he asked himself. She knew nothing of genetics, so why this sudden interest in zygotes? It was true that he and Sam were opposite-handed and parted their hair on different sides. But that didn't mean they were 'mirror images', did it?

It didn't mean they shared the same genes either, or that one of them was a voided half: a shadow foetus cast off before birth, second out of the womb, second for the rest of his life, remaindered. It couldn't mean that, could it? And if it did, *which* of them was second – him or Sam? Funny the way their mother would never tell.

He didn't like the thoughts spiralling through his mind. But he couldn't stop them. Had Sam not always been the one who followed him, tracking him, shading him, imitating, standing in, taking his place, taking over, coveting whatever Jack said or did? Ever since the beginning when Sam copied his picture of the horse that had won the Cheltenham Gold Cup when they were five. Or stole the photo of the whale. Or, later again, at boarding school, when Sam grabbed the lead part in the annual play while Jack was having bones bruised on the rugby pitch, and robbed Jack's place in the hearts of their favourite mentors, Dom Cilian and Abbot Anselm. But the worst of all was over women. First Mary Murphy the baby-sitter, then Violaine the French au pair. Their cousin Maggie Kiely. And then Raphaëlle. Of all the stolen loves, that was the one for which Jack couldn't forgive Sam. The one unpardonable theft. The sin against the Spirit. The way Sam had manoeuvred and contrived behind Jack's back, as they holidayed together those last summers, to take Raphaëlle from him. The way he'd used the cover of novitiate chastity and mystical allusion to win Raphaëlle over, to seduce her soul. Jack hadn't known at the time, of course, suspecting nothing at all until he discovered everything the night that Sam was buried at the abbey and Jack read his diary and learned of his fantasies about Raphaëlle. That was when the terrible doubts began to writhe and coil in the pit of his being.

As he sat against the bedrest and gazed upon Raphaëlle's

prints he felt an interloper in another's space, an excluded middle, stranger to a secret. Raphaëlle's secret this time.

He rose from the bed and paced the room. He went to the window and opened the wooden shutters. They made a little clatter as he pushed them apart, letting in a flow of night breeze. He stood there, breathing through his open mouth for a few minutes, to calm himself, to empty his mind. But it didn't work. Even as he stared out into the St Gallen night, a shadow shot across his face. There was a throbbing in his head. Why had Raphaëlle isolated the diagram of intermediate twins like that? Why had she so deliberately inflated the proportions, so obviously amplified the contours, printing the term 'superfecundation' in bold, even adding the curious phrase 'rare but not unknown'? And what had prompted her to cite Irish birth-rates and the haemoglobin syndrome of red-and-white twins? Jack red, Sam white? Surely Raphaëlle wasn't thinking that Sam and he were fathered by different men? Or worse – much worse – that Sam and he had fathered the same child? Emilie the child of an intermediate pair: himself and Sam? A single ovum of the same cycle fertilised by different brothers? Red and white, reddish white, whitish-red? Preposterous!

He could feel waves, black, vertiginous waves, rise up inside him, recurring surges scalding the back of his throat like bile, making his head spin. He sat down on the chair by the window, but the feeling worsened. The room and everything in it began to twist free from its fixed place and slide out of focus, as if nothing were held within its frame any more, not the violets within the frosted vase, not the pillows within the covers, not the sheets within the blankets, not the prints within the folder. Each thing had lost its centre and floated through a gap, an emptiness less matter than matterlessness, an invisible, hollow space.

He closed his eyes and gripped the arms of his chair

and clung like a drowning man, and stayed immobile for
several minutes, gripping more and more tightly, until the
waves subsided and the fear went away and his palms grew
cool again and he could open his eyes.

4 ∫

Jack reached for the phone and asked reception for long distance. He called Danièle. There was no reply. Just the sing-song of her answering machine. He put down the receiver and turned brusquely towards the window, his face muscles tensed. It was dark outside. No noise rose from the street. He relaxed. What would he say to Danièle had she been there? And what could she say to him? They were in different worlds now.

He lay on the bed, switched off the lamp and tried to sleep. But a faint noise kept coming and going, voices and whispers and sighs, he couldn't tell from where at first; he couldn't even be sure that they were not in his head. Then he heard something move and realised it was from the next room, Emilie's room. She must still be awake.

He put his light back on and, slipping his coat over his pyjamas, went to see if she was all right.

The TV was on. 'What are you watching?' he asked.

'*Rien.*' Emilie sat against a bank of pillows, remote control in hand. Freckled and perky as ever. She was wearing another of her T-shirts as a nightdress, white this time and extra large. Her eyes were wide and quick, focusing on the flickering screen. She didn't look up.

Jack recognised the news channel. 'Why don't you watch something else?'

'*Les autres sont chiants. Même le porno . . .*'

'Porno?' Jack repeated the word.

'*Oui. Por-no.*' She put mock emphasis on each syllable, rolling her 'r' along the roof of her palate. '*Mais t'inquiète pas. Il faut payer pour voir la fin.*'

'*La fin!* What do you mean – *la fin*?'

'*Tu sais . . . l'orgasme,*' she replied matter-of-factly, still staring at the screen.

Jack shuffled over to the TV and pressed the button. He placed his two hands on top of the monitor and forbade Emilie to watch that channel again; he'd speak to Herr Müller first thing in the morning about installing a video recorder instead.

Emilie did not raise her eyes from the blank screen as he made his way from the room, switching the lights off as he went and almost spilling the vase of bird's-foot violets.

'Sleep well,' he said.

Emilie said nothing.

She has Sam's mouth, he thought as he brushed his teeth back in his room, but the colour of her hair is mine. Russet brown, auburn, curly, just like mine when I was a boy.

5

Herr Müller apologised the next morning when Jack spoke to him. It was quite impossible, he explained, to monitor minors' use of the multi-channel facility in the rooms. He looked down at Emilie standing beside Jack at the reception desk in a blue T-shirt and jeans, a brazen look on her face as she twisted an elastic hair bob about her fingers. Müller offered to replace the TV with a VHS and gave Jack the name of a video library in Moosbruggstrasse with a good youth section. He also handed Jack a list of eleven calls made from Emilie's room the previous evening – all to Geneva.

Jack thanked him and put the list in his pocket. Emilie shrugged her shoulders and puckered her lips. Jack asked who she'd rung.

'*Grandmère*,' she replied.

'Eleven times?' said Jack.

'*J'ai aussi appelé mes amies.*' Her face took on a pinched look, a moodiness clouding her charcoal eyes. Not wishing to make a fuss in front of Müller, Jack left it at that.

Much time was spent haggling over tapes in the video store. Jack proposed children's classics, Jacques Tati and *La Grande Vadrouille*. Emilie preferred *The Terminator* and *Evil Dead II*. They settled eventually for *Rattle and Hum* and *Sophie's Choice*.

When Jack left the hotel for Pema Spielereine's, he was

satisfied that Emilie was quite content sitting watching a video in the Müller's downstairs apartment waiting for their daughter to come home. It was nearly midday. His step was almost jaunty as he made his way to the bus stop. The edge had gone from his early morning nerves thanks to a quick jar before leaving his room – three swallows of Scotch from the bottle he'd hidden in his wardrobe.

But once on the bus he found himself fretting again. He was regretting now having brought Emilie to St Gallen without having first made certain that Raphaëlle was there. He really didn't know what to do with a pre-teenage daughter he hardly knew, who should be at school. He had no handle on this new generation, his own experience being confined to growing up with Sam in the shaded groves of a Cork middle-class suburb where the nearest thing to the big bad world was mitching in the Coliseum cinema, learning the facts of life from the Mayfield gang or catcalling prostitutes coming up Beale's Lane from the docks below. That was eleven-year-old boys from Cork; Emilie was an eleven-year-old girl from Geneva.

What would J.J. Toland have done, Jack wondered, if he had found himself wandering about like this with an adolescent daughter he hardly knew in a city whose dialect he hardly spoke? But Toland never had a wife and child and he spoke ten languages – including fluent German. That was the difference. But then again, thought Jack, maybe there were two Tolands wandering around the Continent in the eighteenth century, one with a wife and child, the other without. Maybe that was why his namesake could write a hundred books and appear in so many places – because there was more than one of him. That would make for a nice heading for his thesis, Jack thought: *The Ubiquity of John John Toland*.

He peered out of the window of the bus at the people in the streets, heavily clad for the unseasonal cold, and pulled his collar up about his neck, even though it was warm inside. He'd be at Pema's within minutes. A car backfired passing the bus at traffic lights and Jack jumped. But he settled back again as the vehicle gathered pace on Gallusstrasse, the street façades flitting by in a white blur. He was back in motion. He was going somewhere. The way he'd always liked it. Most of his life he'd been on the move. Extravert and athlete in his teens, scholarship student by his twenties, Jack had been someone sure of his future and hungry to get there. When Sam drowned and Jack learned about his brother's betrayal, the future shed its power and folded back into the past. What he learned about Sam became a crucial part of him, an invisible creature growing inside, swallowing the air of the present, poisoning his fantasies. His passion for high trees and high achievements became a different kind of longing, a lust for things beyond himself. Hidden, forfeited, inaccessible things. Things that belonged to others. Sam's enigmas. His namesake's codes and cyphers. Raphaëlle's secrets.

6

Jack found the house in a suburban terrace fronted by generous gardens. He opened the gate marked 27 and passed by a white wrought-iron table and chairs protected from the street by a four-foot hedge, then along a paved stone path under a small oak tree, just coming into leaf. *Quercus robur*. Approaching the door, he caught sight of a woman through the front window, seated at a desk, her back to him, speaking on the phone. He presumed it was Pema Spielereine and decided to wait until she'd finished her call before ringing the bell. She wore her hair bobbed. Jack's eyes fastened on the nape of her neck, luminously exposed between a low-cut collar and a neat chignon of dark hair pulled up at the back. He wished she'd feel his eyes burning her skin and turn around. But she didn't, and he still couldn't bring himself to ring. Something about her not turning around paralysed him, fixed him to the spot. The lure of a woman's neck. Like Yahweh seen from behind. The 'she' that Raphaëlle spoke of in her workbook?

The woman put down the receiver and, rising from her seat, turned in Jack's direction. Hair cropped tight in a pudding-bowl fringe, eyes too small for her broad pale face and wide chin.

Jack rang the bell, and she opened the door.

'Pema Spielereine?'

'Yes,' she said opening the door wider.

'Jack Toland.' He held his hand out. 'I'm Raphaëlle's husband.'

Pema shook his hand.

'Is she here?' Jack nodded past her towards the interior of the house.

'She's not.'

'Can you tell me where she is?'

'I'm afraid I can't.' She turned for a moment to adjust a pot of red-and-white geraniums suspended on the wall beside her.

'But you're her friend, you must have some idea.' Jack shuffled from foot to foot. 'I know she's been coming here to work with you.'

Pema hesitated.

'I came all the way here to talk with her. Our daughter, Emilie, came too. She's back at the hotel. May I come in for a moment?'

Pema held his gaze for a moment, as if looking through him to the back of his skull, then pulled the door back. 'All right,' she said, 'but only for a few minutes. I have someone coming at ten thirty.'

Jack stepped past her into the hall. He felt gauche. He'd been expecting someone Raphaëlle's age and couldn't see how this odd little woman, twice her years, could be the 'she' of Raphaëlle's most intimate reflections.

She led him through a library-cum-lobby into a simply furnished room and ushered him towards an armchair flanked by beaded cushions. The room was bathed in a fragrance of musk and incense.

'What exactly can I do for you?' she asked, sitting on a low couch opposite, her legs crossed under her.

'Help me find my wife.'

'I must make it clear right away, Mr Toland, my relationship with Raphaëlle is professional. I'm not permitted to speak about it.'

Jack put up his hands and nodded. 'OK. But I'm worried about her. At least tell me if she's safe.'

'She's safe.' Pema tugged at the sides of her cotton skirt and rearranged her seating position. 'But you need to let her be right now. Trust her.'

'Look, if you can't tell me where she is, surely you can tell me this – was she working with you on the twins book?'

'In a way.' Pema poured mint tea from a pottery jug. 'At first, at any rate.'

'I don't understand,' said Jack, watching Pema's hands move deftly over the cups.

'What began as research became another kind of search.' She offered Jack a cup without elaborating.

He drank.

She watched, relaxed, studying him gently with her small eyes. Her lips thinned into a half-smile.

Jack hoisted his leg sideways, releasing the clasp with a quick flick, and pulled himself back into a straight posture. He stared at Pema. 'I know Raphaëlle is dedicating the book to you.'

She nodded.

'What brought her here in the first place?'

'She was on a work visit, photographing a diptych of two Irish monks.'

'Gallus and Columbanus?'

'Something like that.' She sipped from her steaming cup. 'It was for her book.'

'Yes,' Jack said. 'I've seen it in the folio. The publisher gave me a copy when I met him two days ago.' He swallowed a mouthful of tea.

'The Basilica,' Pema continued. 'That's where I met her. Quite by accident really. Last October. I was showing some students round the Klosterhof.'

'Are you a teacher?'

She smiled, shook her head.

'A therapist?' His eyes slid sideways, trying to take in some telltale item in the room.

'You could say that.' She looked down briefly at her hands in her lap, as if considering whether she should say more, then raised her eyes towards Jack. 'I was a missionary for years, a Sister of Charity working in the Sudan. There was a lot of famine at the time, cholera and people dying. It was hard. When I returned I left the order and took up training as a counsellor, Jungian mainly, at the Zurich Institute.'

'So, why would Raphaëlle talk to you about twins?' Jack ran his fingers over the handle of his stick.

Pema didn't answer. She picked up the pot and gestured towards Jack's empty cup. He handed it to her. She poured, then changed her sitting position, tucking both legs more tightly under her and folding her arms over her chest. She spoke in a single flow, the animation of her words consorting oddly with her tranquil pose. 'First time we met, in the Basilica, we spoke a lot, hours in fact. It began as a chance conversation about the ceiling portrait of Gallus and Columbanus, then turned into a lengthy exchange in a small café in Webergstrasse. Raphaëlle took my card that afternoon and returned to visit me here days later. That was late October. She came to talk about her work on Gemini, bringing her collection of prints with her. She wanted to make connections between the images, the ones for her book. She came back several times.'

Jack gestured to her to go on. But she didn't. After a moment's silence, she leaned forward and said: 'That's as much as I can tell you.'

Jack scrutinised her features and clothes as if they might betray what her words would not; the sharp nose and eyes shrouded in solemnity, the deep lines running from her nostrils to the corners of her lips, her frail hands and miniature feet, her handmade sandals and light Indian cotton skirt, her smell of musk, her voice of velvet. But the more he looked the more sibylline she appeared, until her Buddha-like pose and unflappable composure began to rankle. 'I have to find her,' he said tightly. 'Why can't you give me some idea where she is?'

'I'm sorry.'

'I must talk to her.' Jack reached for his cigarettes, but Pema said she'd prefer if he didn't smoke. She had other people to see. She looked down at her wristwatch and explained that her next appointment was in ten minutes.

'All right,' he said, putting his cigarette pack back in his pocket. 'I accept that you won't say where Raphaëlle is, but there must be something you can do to help me. You're my only connection to her.' His voice was jittery with desperation.

'Come back tomorrow,' said Pema. 'I have a free hour between ten and eleven in the morning. But I promise nothing.'

'I know,' said Jack, pressing his palms to his knees and rising from his chair. 'Thank you.'

As they passed through the hallway on the way out, Jack paused to inspect a pair of sculpted ornaments on the table by the coatrack. Two insects. One like a minuscule extraterrestrial, cut in two. The other a scorpion, also bisected. 'You're admiring my cleft creature,' said Pema, handing Jack his coat. 'I brought them back from the Sudan.'

'What are they?'

'They're Yoruban twin-signs. The first is a nasty piece of nature. A replica of the bulldog ant. When split in half, a battle takes place between the head and tail.'

'And this one?' Jack held the glinting obsidian scorpion in the palm of his hand. He raised it to eye level.

'That's a cult object.' Pema's voice was relaxed now, so different from the formal tone in her room. 'In certain West African tribes, the sundered scorpion represents the mutation of the first woman's clitoris into a creature with eight feet. A symbol of two newborn infants with their sum of eight arms and legs. Curious, no?'

'Yes,' muttered Jack, his eyes trained on the sculpted piece. He juggled it nervously from hand to hand. It was heavy for such a small object.

'The scorpion protected twins. No one dared touch it for fear of its sting.' Pema held her palm out. 'Raphaëlle gave it to me.'

'Raphaëlle! She really *was* obsessed,' said Jack, handing the figurine back to her. So Raphaelle was still thinking of him. And Sam, of course. But was it one of them or both. And if one, which one?

Pema took the scorpion without saying anything. She shook Jack's hand and held the door open. He noticed a small tattoo on the inside of her outstretched wrist but couldn't make it out.

'Tomorrow at ten, then,' he said.

'Tomorrow at ten.'

7

Out on the street, a bitter breeze was shearing off the southern slopes of the Alps and sweeping through the city. The sky was cloudless, a bowl of bright crescent moon rising in the pale daylight blue. Snow had not descended on the valley after all. But there was ice in the air.

As he waited for a bus to town, Jack pulled the hood of his duffel coat over his head, like a novice cowling a tonsured pate. Tipping a cigarette from his pack, he lit up, sucked deep, and prayed the bus would hurry. He leaned against the wall under a beech branching on to the street from an adjoining garden; the wind was like a knife.

He was confused and frustrated. Pema Spielereine wouldn't answer his questions, but she'd managed to pitch something into the pool of his mind and he was curious to see where the ripples led. Spielereine clearly knew more than she was saying and, besides, she was his only clue. He'd gain her confidence and see what he could find out.

8 ∫

When Jack walked into the lobby of the hotel, Herr Müller handed him another print-out.

'I think you should see this, Mr Toland,' he said courteously.

Jack looked. The same list of eleven calls he'd seen that morning.

'Of course, I'll pay,' Jack assured him.

'You do not understand, Mr Toland.' Müller removed his wire-frame glasses to stare at Jack with tired eyes. 'I know you will pay. It's the amount . . .'

'The amount?'

'Yes. It is the second time your daughter rings these numbers. This morning, after her video, she complained of a headache to my wife who brought her up to her room to lie down. She spent over an hour on the phone. Each call comes through the switchboard. I thought you should know.'

'I'll talk to her.' Jack tapped his stick on the floor. 'It won't happen again.'

'It's not me I'm thinking of. It's your bill, Mr Toland.'

'I appreciate that,' said Jack, stuffing the phone list into his breast pocket. He asked Müller to block all future calls as he limped towards the stairwell. Halfway up the first flight he turned around.

'Is Emilie in her room?'

'Yes. She's with Margarita. I suggested they play down-stairs, but your daughter wanted to watch one of the videos you chose.'

Both girls were propped up on Emilie's bed, shoes off, when Jack entered the room. Engrossed in a video, they hardly acknowledged his arrival. He walked to the centre of the room, partially blocking the monitor. Emilie, wearing an extra-large shirt, looked up at him and asked: *'Tu as trouvé Maman?'*

'No,' Jack replied. 'Not yet.'

'Tu es nul.' Emilie turned back to the screen and motioned him aside with a wave of the remote control. When he didn't move, she gave a drawl of protest. *'Papa, c'est la meilleure partie du film!'*

'Aren't you going to introduce me to your friend?' he said. Emilie didn't look up. She toyed with the control in her hands for a moment, then pressed the off button.

Jack swivelled his head in time to catch the fleeting face of Meryl Streep diminish to a tiny white square. *Sophie's Choice.* The screen went blank.

'My name is Margarita,' said the Müller girl, holding up her hand from her reclining position on the bed for Jack to shake.

'Pleased to meet you,' said Jack. He took her hand and shook it before adding, 'I need to speak to Emilie alone for a moment.'

'J'ai pas de secrets.' Emilie glared.

'All right', he said, trying a severe voice. 'Why are you phoning your friends, Emilie?'

'J'avais promis . . .'

'You promised what?'

'J'avais promis de les tenir tous au courant chaque jour de ce que je faisais.' Her tone was matter-of-fact.

'It's private,' said Jack.

'J'ai déjà tout dit à mes amies.'

'What do you mean, *tout*?'

'*Tout.*' She continued to look at the empty video screen. '*Les disputes. L'alcoolisme. Les drogues. La séparation. Que Maman est partie. Que t'es revenu après cinq ans.*'

'You mean you told everyone in your class everything . . .'

'*Oui. Même que tu es monopède.*'

'*Monopède?*'

'*Quelqu'un qui n'a qu'un pied.*'

'I know what you mean. It's just no one ever called me that before.'

'*Et alors!*'

Jack turned his back to the girls, facing the video screen. He flinched at what he saw. There, under the monitor, propping it up the extra few inches needed for Emilie and Margarita to get a full view of the screen while lying on the bed, was a staggered pile of his Toland editions with, top of the pile, the 1696 first edition of *Christianity Not Mysterious*. There was a broad black burn across the edge of the cover.

He bent down and scrutinised the shape of the burn; it was caused by a cigarette. The two girls had been smoking in the room. That was why both windows on to the street were open wide. Margarita coolly volunteered that most of the girls in her class smoked.

'Let's get out of here.' Jack threw a hand up in exasperation. 'Let's go visit a museum.'

'*Ah non!*' said Emilie.

'*Ah si!*' said Jack. He made towards the door, expecting them to follow.

'*Attends Margarita quand même,*' Emilie shouted, making him wait while Margarita took some things from under the pillow – nail varnish, eye pencil, cigarettes, photos – and threw them into her satchel before joining them for the walk.

9

Jack asked at reception for a tourist map and listings of museums and other sites in St Gallen. Herr Müller handed him a fold-out brochure which included a street map, but informed him that some museums were closed on Wednesdays. Margarita and Emilie said they wanted to go swimming instead and Müller suggested Jack take the girls to the municipal *Schwimbad*. It was open to the public until six and was only three streets away. Margarita ran off to get swimsuits, lending one to Emilie. They headed off to the pool, arm in arm, towels and togs over their shoulders. Both mimicked a raucous rock song with English words – *Lover I'm off the streets, gonna go where the bright lights and the big city meet with a red guitar, on fire, desire.* Jack struggled to keep up as the girls sauntered past the old brasseries, bookstores, cafés, shoe shops, restaurants and fragrant bakeries that lined the commercial and residential streets of the Aldstadt. It was mid-afternoon and the air was pink-hazed. Jack felt well for the first time since he'd arrived in the town.

The girls slipped into the dressing room as he climbed to the visitors' gallery overlooking the pool. He sat and inhaled. He loved the smell of chlorine. The sharp, clean fumes. Ever since he used to swim in the Eglinton baths in Cork every Monday afternoon with Sam and his class from Christian Brothers College. Every week of term from

the age of six to the age of twelve, when he left to board
at Columbanus Abbey. It took just the slightest whiff of
the heavy-smelling gas for him to be back beneath the
tepid water, lips and nostrils blowing out the tangy liquid
as his head rose above the surface. Best of all after a
deep dive, when his lungs sucked hungrily at the close,
pungent air.

He watched as Emilie and Margarita skipped from
the ladies' changing room like two svelte ballerinas and
plunged into the pool. They turned and dipped in the
water, shrieking in the echoing domed space and pausing
for breath every so often at the side bars, their skinny
bottoms pushed out behind them as they chattered and
laughed.

Jack leaned back in his seat and was about to risk a quick
smoke when two other people came up to the gallery. He
put his unlit cigarette back in the packet and lay back
for a nap.

A high-pitched cry shook him from his slumber. Margarita screaming Emilie's name. He leaned forward in his seat
to see Emilie floating face down in the water, immobile,
lifeless. He must save her! His body sprang upwards but
his leg stayed put, sending him headlong into the gallery
aisle. He struggled to his feet, helped by his neighbours, and
rubbed a bruised elbow. He peered over the gallery rail. It
hardly seemed a minute since his fall, but he couldn't see
Emilie now. The cool blue surface of the pool was still. He
called her name, once, twice. No answer. He felt separated
from everyone in the pool by some invisible, dumb light,
as if he were gazing through the glass of an aquarium.

'Papa.' He spun around to see Emilie and Margarita
standing behind him, dripping, towels over their heads.
They were smiling.

'*C'était une blague!*' said Emilie.

'It wasn't funny,' he said, trying to hide the fear in
his face.

On the way back to the hotel, he found himself walking alone with Emilie. Margarita had gone to collect a friend and Emilie sauntered along beside him, pulling her towel from one shoulder to the other as if it were a scarf. He wanted to say something to her about Sam, about his drowning in Poul Gorm, about how deeply it had marked his life. But he realised it was unspeakable. Like a silent hole left in water after someone falls in, frozen at that split moment, that moment of splitting, before the waves come rushing back to fill the gap, to make the surface whole again. Poul Gorm. Yes, the place of the blue-black hole. A frozen place in a frozen present, an instant suspended beyond memory, an experience never experienced.

He wanted to tell Emilie things about the past, things that happened before she was born. He glanced at his daughter. 'I know how hard it is for you,' he said as they strolled up Weberstrasse, side by side. 'Waiting around in this strange city while I'm trying to find your mother.'

She didn't look up while he spoke but continued pulling her towel back and forth across her shoulders and neck.

'It must have been confusing for you, the break-up.' He looked down at their feet walking in step beside each other, Emilie's pace deliberately halting, off cue. 'I was always convinced it was best for all of us. I was impossible then, destroying everything and everyone around me. I even stopped believing in your mother, the only woman I've loved.' He swallowed. He felt awkward speaking of such things. He gave Emilie a sidelong glance to see if she might ask him to explain, but she didn't. 'I hope,' he said, mumbling his words, 'we'll find your mother soon.' He cleared his throat and slowed to a halt.

Emilie continued for a step or two before stopping and looking back at him.

'I'll try to make things up to you, Emilie. I promise,' he said.

She did not respond. But, after a moment standing there not moving, a shiver ran across her cheek like the luffing of a stretched white sail.

10

After supper, Emilie and Margarita watched Margarita's favourite TV show in the Müllers' downstairs flat. *Silvia Seidel*, it was called, about a sixteen-year-old ballerina who becomes paralysed and loses her boyfriend. Jack sat up in his room finishing his last half-bottle and wondering why the hell Raphaëlle had given those African insects to Pema. He had a bad feeling in his bones about them. Then he recalled seeing a sequence of African images in her folio. He reached across to where it still lay by his bed from the previous evening, and opened it at the print of a Dogan double cup. He gazed at the image until his eyes hurt; the two round scoops, joined at the edge like an open oyster-shell, and perched upon a wide uterine oil jar painted with tiny figures of scorpions and bull ants. On the opposite page he read:

Cosmogenic tales of doubling are most common in Africa. Of these, the most famous is the Dogon tradition which recounts how in the beginning there were eight original pairs. Four women who were both female and male with the female dominant; and four men who were both male and female with the male dominant. They mated with themselves, each female part of each pair becoming pregnant and generating children. Since the original heavenly powers were dual, and intervened in mortals' affairs in the guise of twins, the worst blasphemy was to say God was One. In the Holy Time of the Great Beginning, everything came into existence in twos, human and divine. Dogon twin-births were the occasion of ritual practices where the infants were shaved by adult twins who put special double cups on the altar of their ancestors. Scorpion-shaped strips of leather were consecrated by a blood sacrifice of eight birds, and made into pendants which the twin children wore around their necks. The Dogon tradition also held that economic trade began with twins. As the two scoops of the double cup were equal, so twins were interchangeable. Selling and buying things was exchanging twins.

In the Yoruba tradition of western Nigeria, everyone had a double in heaven. This Sky Double enacted whatever corresponded to the actions of the earth-child below. Twin-birth was seen as an earthly manifestation of this spiritual doubling. When twins were born, it was assumed that one of them was meant for heaven, one for earth; but since it was impossible to tell which was which, both were honoured as equally 'sky-blessed'. At birth, their mother sang to them: 'You are the ones who open doors in heaven, who open doors on earth.' Each pair, irrespective of sex, was named Twaiwo ('he who has first taste of the world') and Kehinde ('he who lags behind'). The first-born, Twaiwo, was attributed qualities of spontaneity, daring and quick-wittedness. The second-born, Kehinde, possessed the contrasting qualities of wisdom and caution. Though Twaiwo was first out of the womb, he was considered junior to Kehinde.

The incidence of twin-births is high in the Yoruba tribe – twice that of any other people in the world; so also is the rate of infant mortality. When any of the twins die, the parents have a local carver make a wood surrogate (ere ibeji) *which they then proceed to clothe, feed and tend as they would a living child. If the living twin is scarred or bruised, a similar mark is given to the proxy image. These wooden statuettes, or in more recent times photographs and plastic dolls, are very powerful; if their sky-bonded doubleness is not honoured, they unleash dangerous forest demons and bestial forces of disorder. The local priest of the tribe determines how long the care of the surrogate twin should last. 'Everyone has a spirit twin,' the Yoruba tradition holds. 'The vanishing twin is the twin within. When you meet yourself, you will be happy all the time. Wherever you go, there you are.'*

Jack sat back and envisaged the little cleft creatures at Pema's. The split scorpion with eight feet. Pema must have given Raphaëlle the idea for this passage. They must have worked on it together. But what did it mean to live without your double?

Some believe these African traditions of twinship have been influenced by myths from the East. Often cited is the Indian creation myth of the Rig Veda which recounts the birth of brother-sister twins, Yama and Yami, after their substitute mother was impregnated by the Sun. Yama and Yami coupled incestuously to found the human race. When Yama died, Yami was so inconsolable that the gods contrived to create the time of day and night. With the passing of each day into yesterday, the danger Yami's grief posed to the world began to fade. Wisdom was learning to live without your double.

Egyptian mythology may also have been an influence; in particular the famous tale of the solar/lunar twins, Isis and Nephythys. They were born together with brother twins, Set and Osiris. When Osiris died and disappeared, his sibling and future bride, Isis, went to great lengths to resurrect him from the dead – retrieving her double from the underworld.

Jack slammed the folio shut. What was Raphaëlle up to with these vanishing doubles and spirit twins, all this odd African lore about the second-born being wiser than the first, surrogates replacing originals, powers of primogeniture? Was she still wondering, after all these years, what it might have been like with Sam had he never drowned, had she lived with him instead of with Jack? Were these the things she was working through during her visits to Pema?

He put the prints back in his bag, grabbed the remote control and channel-hopped for an hour or so. He tried watching a local programme called *Die Glückliche Familie* but switched off after ten minutes. He rang Danièle in Montreal, then Belle-Mère in Geneva; no reply from either number. He even took out his Toland books, smelled the sealed leather covers and stained pages, spread them wide on his bed and stared at each one. But he couldn't concentrate, not now, snagged and bound as he was, locked in the penitentiary of his own doubt.

11

Around 10 p.m. Jack heard Emilie going to bed next door. She didn't look in to say goodnight, so Jack went out into the corridor and knocked. She told him to come in. He did. She was sitting up on her bed with a pencil and paper, drawing or writing, Jack could not be sure. He didn't enquire.

'*Ça va?*' she asked.

'Fine,' said Jack. He sank heavily into an upholstered chair by the window and took out a cigarette. Emilie asked if he wouldn't mind opening a shutter and using the ashtray by the bedroom sink. 'For an underage smoker you have your rules!' he said. He lit up and inhaled.

Emilie spoke first. '*Tu as des nouvelles de Maman?*'

'Not yet,' he said. 'But I'm hoping to get some leads from Frau Spielereine.' He paused to exhale smoke through his nostrils. 'Tomorrow.'

'*Tu lui as demandé où Maman était allée?*'

'She doesn't answer things like that.'

'*Pourquoi?*'

'I don't know'.

'*Et qu'est ce que tu faisais ce soir?*'

'I worked in my room,' he lied.

'*Tu bossais?*'

'Yes.' He twisted towards the table beside him and stubbed out his cigarette. 'I'm working on an Irish scientist. I've been working on him since I went to Montreal.' He looked back at Emilie and smiled. 'The book you burnt yesterday. That was one of his.'

'C'est un livre de quoi?' Her voice was curt but curious.

'Science and religion.'

'Pourquoi religion?'

'Because the man who wrote it, J.J. Toland, believed that religious mysteries aren't really mysteries at all.' He paused. 'Once we get to know what's behind them.'

'Il a le même nom que toi.'

'Yes.' Jack moved from the chair and sat at the foot of Emilie's bed. 'It's funny really,' he said, 'the way his first names changed all the time. He was christened Janus Junius, that's a Roman name, but in Irish this became Seán Eoin – Seán is from the Norman Jehan, and Eoin from the Latin Johannes. When he went to school and began to speak in English, this became John John.' He tapped the wooden base of Emilie's bed with a flourish. 'So that's why, to avoid confusion, I always refer to him by his initials – J.J.'

'C'est ridicule tout ça!' Emilie rolled her eyes to heaven. She put down her pencil and looked at him.

'Maybe.' He smiled. 'But names matter.'

'Toi aussi tu as changé ton nom?'

'Not really. I was christened John, and Jack is short for John.'

'Mais c'est pas plus court! Les deux noms ont quatre lettres!'

'I mean short as in a nickname.'

Emilie picked up her pencil again and began to write something on her notepad.

'De toutes façons, je n'aime pas le nom Toland,' she said, throwing Jack a pert look. *'C'est moche.'* The words flew from her mouth like a spray of little birds.

'It's your name too . . .'

'Non, je m'appelle Emilie Feher-Feldring maintenant. Maman a changé mon nom pour son nom quand tu es parti pour Montréal.'

'She never told me . . .' He felt winded by the hurt of it; he didn't finish his sentence.

'*Pourquoi elle te l'aurait dit?*' Emilie's eyes flashed. '*Tu n'étais pas là!*' She pressed her shoulders back against the carved headrest of the bed, wrinkling her nose and lowering her head to her pad. Then she added, in a quieter tone, as if to take the hurt away: '*Comment va ta jambe?*'

'My leg's fine,' said Jack. He smiled and patted Emilie's foot as he rose from the end of the bed. He paused to look down at the sketchbook in her lap and asked, 'What's that?'

'*Notre jardin.*' She turned the drawing around so that he could get a proper look.

'The different flowers?'

She nodded. '*Je connais les couleurs, mais pas les noms.*'

'I'll tell you them if you like. I planted most of them.'

She brushed her hair back with her hand. '*D'accord.*' She pointed to a blue-and-white flower.

'Hibiscus.'

Then to multi-petalled red ones.

'Hydrangea.'

Then tubular pinks all dappled inside.

'Foxgloves.'

Then tiny purple cups.

'Blue flax.'

And emerald-green pointed leaves.

'Wisteria. And those trees at the back, behind the garden bench, they're cherries and willows.'

Emilie looked up, impressed, and asked him if he knew the names in French.

'Afraid not,' he said. 'But I can name them in Latin if you like.'

She nodded, amused, and Jack recited the names of each flower and shrub and tree, ending with his favourites – *Prunus kurielensis, Salix caprea pendula.*

'*C'est chouette ça!*' said Emilie with a broad grin. She sat up against the pillows and asked him to repeat every name, letter by letter, so that she could write them under each plant in her drawing.

In between each name, she asked him lots of different questions. How he came to know all these terms, and how long ago it had been that he had planted the trees in their garden, and why he preferred this tree to that, or Raphaëlle preferred that flower to this. And Jack told her, recalling as he did how much he'd loved botany when studying science at Cork University, how he and Sam would walk the forests of Columbanus Abbey with their abbot and learn all the names of the oaks and redwoods, how he and Raphaëlle had spent almost every weekend during their first year together in Cork collecting and photographing specimens from local woods for Jack's research.

By the time Emilie had heard all this and had finally filled in all the Latin names, it was almost midnight. Jack tapped his wristwatch and said she must go to sleep immediately.

'*Bonne nuit,*' he said as he slipped the switch and left the room.

'Goodnight', said Emilie. It was only when he was out in the corridor that he realised it was the first time she'd spoken to him in English.

An hour later, before turning off his own lights, Jack went
back to Emilie's room to see if she was asleep. She was.
But her earphones were still wrapped around her head
and the tape was still on. Must be a habit, he thought, as
he removed them without disturbing her. Before pressing
'off', he lifted one of the small sponge speakers to his ear
and listened. A cracked smoky voice sang about fireflies
and locusts and Jacob wrestling with an angel until the
angel was overcome and a demon seed was planted and
a flower of fire raised up. Hard rock, too hard for Jack just
now. He turned off the tape and placed the Walkman on
Emilie's side table beside the vase of flowers. Returning to
his room, he took his last bottle from its hiding place under
his clothes in the cupboard and, without undressing, drank
himself to sleep.

'Where did you find those earrings?' Jack asked Emilie across the breakfast table.

'Margarita gave them to me,' she said. She fingered the plastic rubies at the base of each ear and assumed one of her puckered frowns. He held back a smile: she was still speaking English.

They ate in silence for several minutes until Emilie put down her spoon and pushed her bowl of cereal away. 'Papa, I want to leave.' Her eyes flickered like dark coals. 'I don't want to be in this hotel any more,' she said, 'watching videos and reading Tintin and not being able to ring my friends – or to find Maman.' Her words were hard as hail.

Jack sat at the table under the louvred windows of the hotel dining room and listened. His tongue felt dry and rough in his mouth, though he'd already drunk two orange juices. Emilie was right. Their second day in St Gallen and he hadn't gotten anywhere. Not the smallest hint of where Raphaëlle might be staying; the twins stuff was a cul-de-sac; Pema's cryptic remarks bewildering; his suspicions of Raphaëlle deepening. If something didn't turn up today, he'd take Emilie back to Geneva.

'We'll go soon,' he promised, pushing his own break-fast plate away from him. 'I've arranged to meet Pema Spielereine once more this morning. If nothing comes of it this time we'll leave immediately. I promise. We'll take the evening train to Geneva.'

'Can I go to Pema's with you?' she asked.

'I'm sorry. I need to talk to her alone. But you'll be fine with the Müllers, won't you?' He ran a starched napkin across his lips and rose from the table. 'I'll be back by lunch-time.'

'I'll be fine,' said Emilie. She bent her head and finished her breakfast alone.

14

On the bus to Pema's, Jack sat at the rear, one hand nervously rubbing the crown of his head. He stared through the window without focusing on the passing streets. All he could feel now was one pain-stab after another shoot across his forehead. He'd have to watch the drink.

As the bus approached Gallusstrasse, he thought he recognised someone standing on the corner. Yes, he was certain as he pressed his face to the window pane – it was Margarita Müller talking to a man on the pavement by the Stiftspark. The man seemed familiar too, but Jack couldn't place him. As the bus drew level, he looked again and thought he was seeing things. It was him surely, older, greyer, heavier perhaps, but him all right, standing there under a large sycamore. Dr Klaus, Anselm's old novitiate friend from the Klosterhof.

He got off at the next stop and hurried back to the corner. By the time he reached Margarita she was alone. He asked where Klaus was. Klaus? she asked. The man she had been talking to a minute ago was not called Klaus but Bessler, her teacher. They'd just had a sports lesson in the nearby gym. Herr Bessler had gone back to school and she'd have to hurry now, she said, if she wasn't to be late. Jack frowned and looked about him. He must have mistaken the man for someone else, he said apologetically.

As Margarita left, Jack stood on the pavement under a dull, brassy sky. He closed his eyes, opened them again. He stared at his unpolished shoes. He'd really have to watch the drink.

The smell of musk in Pema Spielereine's room was over-powering. Jack searched for something significant to say but couldn't think of anything. He told Pema he and Emilie would be leaving St Gallen later that day unless they got some news of Raphaëlle's whereabouts. A half-smile ghosted across her lips as she ushered him to a chair, offered to take his stick and put it by the door. He tried to get another glimpse of the tattoo on her wrist, but her cotton sleeves came down to her hands.

The meeting began with peppermint tea. Pema, sitting cross-legged on the low couch opposite him prepared two cups. Jack inhaled the aroma of a slowly burning joss-stick then, looking at Pema, he asked, 'Have you spoken to Raphaëlle since we met yesterday?'

'You know I can't talk about Raphaëlle.'

'What's so secret? If it was a man I could understand. But Raphaëlle's mother seems to think it's not.'

She straightened her neck but didn't comment.

'Have you any idea why she asked me to come back?'

Still she did not reply.

Jack leaned forward in his chair. 'She must have said something about Sam and me, about the reason she was obsessed with twins?' He began to raise his voice. 'Look, you know I'm desperate. You're the only person I can talk to. Is there no way you can help me?'

'Yes,' said Pema after a pause. She poured a cup of hot tea and passed it over to him. 'I can teach you what I taught Raphaëlle.'

'What's that?'

'To breathe'.

'*Breathe?* Why breathe?'

'To slow down, to silence the active mind, to let go.'

'Let go of what?' Jack stammered. 'What did Raphaëlle need to let go of?'

'We all need to let go of something.'

'Why?'

'Because if you can't let go of something, you don't possess it, it possesses you.'

'I really don't know what you're saying.'

'That's all right, Jack. Just trust me for a while now. Relax and calm the motions of your mind. Do as I say.'

Jack nodded; he'd come this far, he'd go the extra mile. He followed her instructions one by one. He removed his calliper and sat upright in the high-backed chair, planting the soles of his feet squarely on the carpetless floor. He grasped the hot cup tightly between his hands, letting the warmth penetrate through his fingers and palms. Concentrated so on the local sensation in his hands, he was guided by Pema through a series of somatic shifts, moving his attention punctually from arms and neck down through chest, abdomen and thighs to knees, calves and feet. Having thus released the tension from his body, he was ready, said Pema, for the breathing exercises. This final move involved focusing all senses on the silent inner rhythms of an old Aramaic mantra – *marathana* – inhaling deeply to the pit of his stomach.

'Feel the chair's upright in the small of your back,' said Pema calmly. 'Feel it firm against your spine and shoulder blades and kidneys. Close your eyes and imagine you are lying back into your seat as a plane takes off from a runway.'

He did as she said.

Many things, lost things, grieving things, holy things, things
unvisited for years, came spinning through Jack's mind as he
sat with his eyes closed in Pema's chair, reciting the ancient
mantra and inhaling.

Reciting night petitions to Jesus with Sam, their mother
kneeling by the bed in the high house in Tivoli, her fragrant
presence filling the room, circling like a halo round their
heads, their guardian dear, lighting and guarding, guarding
and lighting. And Mary Murphy, the baby-sitter who knelt
between them too, on other nights in the house by the sea,
the chalet in Myrtleville on the hill above Poul Gorm, Mary
just fifteen years old and a great reciter of bedtime prayers,
even better than their mother, with a deep-sea smell, like
oarwood or iodine for grazed knees, as if she'd just come out
of the ocean, out of the dark bottom of the sea where sugar
kelp and spiral weed flowed in the tide like her hair fanning
out behind when she swam in the cove in the evenings,
before she came to put them to bed when their parents were
away in Cork and showed them her favourite postcards of
Holy Saints and Madonnas with Child, all aquamarine and
luminous and good. Just as she did on that last August night
before she left them for ever to regain the Myrtleville sea,
returning to the belly of the whale that swam beyond the
Ballycotton lighthouse, the whale he and Sam had seen
with their father out fishing the day the rubby-dubby bag

disappeared from the stern of the trawler, shorn in half, a deep morsure through the brown netting. And Jack recalled saying prayers with others too, like Brother Keogh in the primary school in Cork, his shiny soutane flecked with chalk as he struggled to prepare their seven-year-old souls for the Eucharist, telling Genesis stories over and over, like the story of Jacob stealing his brother's birthright, Sam's favourite always, and wrestling with an angel through the desert night, receiving a slash in his side that left him limping for the rest of his days; or rehearsing psalms with Abbot Anselm and the monks, intoning plainchant at Matins and Vespers and verses of John Chrysostum beloved of Cistercians, as Anselm elected Jack, then Sam, then Jack again. Even images of the holy brothers Gall and Columbanus came back, of the *vita sancti Galli* whose portraits on the roof of the Klosterhof oratory Raphaëlle had shown both Jack and Sam on their first visit to St Gallen all those years ago. And thoughts of Toland came back too: his thoughts on God, on space, on matter and the black omnivorous void.

Jack recalled these things in a trance and imagined more besides and spoke some of them aloud to Pema, who sat silent on the wide couch opposite him in that noiseless, half-lit, aromatic room. He felt he should be ridding his mind of images and thoughts, memories and reveries, but instead they came back to him unbidden, like eels to hatching grounds.

Some thirty or forty minutes passed, Jack could not be sure, before he reopened his eyes. As soon as he did, he realised how utterly relaxed he was. Pema sat there with her legs crossed under her, eyes still closed. At first he just looked at her, almost admiring her immobility, her rapt concentration on some silent thing, her look of gentle gravitas. And he almost began to understand how Raphaëlle could have spent so much time with her during all these months, learning to breathe like this, to see like this, to meditate on inner things. Perhaps it was such journeying back through memory which had kindled Raphaëlle's passion for twins. Perhaps it was this exercise of letting go which had exposed her unbroken bond to himself and Sam.

The minutes nudged past, grindingly slow. This might be the sort of New Age thing Charmaine Le Monde would be attracted to, but surely not the Raphaëlle he knew?

As he was having these thoughts, the doorbell rang out in the hallway. Pema opened her eyes slowly and, excusing herself, left the room.

Jack sat on in his chair and stared about him. A small framed mirror on the side table returned an unflattering sight. His thin hair was dishevelled, his eyes jaundiced. He turned away and scanned the nearby bookshelves framed at either end by trompette crystal. The *Jung Codex* and *Answer to Job*. Freud's *Collected Works*. Shakespeare's *Comedy of Errors*. Tao and Eastern mysticism. Heidegger, Meister Eckhart, Hildegarde of Bingen and the Rhine mystics. Irenaeus and Badilides and Coptic Gnostic gospels in thirteen volumes. *Nag Hammadi, Revelation of Adam to Seth, Paraphrase of Shem, The Book of St Thomas*.

He stood up and walked to the bookshelf. He ran his fingers along the spines until he reached the first volume of the *Nag Hammadi* codex. He pulled the leather edition out and opened the introduction. Within seconds, he was skimming, reading how a batch of Hebrew manuscripts was discovered in 1945 in a robber's grave near the town of Nag Hammadi, halfway up the Nile, and presented to Jung as a birthday gift in 1952. His eyes raced on as, turning the pages, he learned of a further seven tractates including the 'Gospel of Thomas', a papyrus censored for hundreds of years and buried underground. The Gospel and Book of Thomas contained revelation dialogues between Jesus and Thomas-Judas concerning the Last Things. Thomas was known as 'Twin', 'Athlete' and 'Contestant' because – along with other outlawed gospelists, Philip, Barnabas and

Magdalen – he posed a real challenge to the Jewish Jesus beloved of the four evangelists and the Church Fathers.

He paused and reread a passage: 'Thomas the Twin proposed a gnosis which denied the separateness of God and declared both good and evil to be substances in the same space. Certain humans – the elect pneumatics – sought this gnosis for themselves by joining together in *likemindedness* and rejecting the moral divisions of the Jewish God. Once they achieved the Knowledge, pneumatics experienced a *resurrection* and became Divine. This involved the return of a twin-partner uniting with its original heavenly image, fusing into one in the angelic order of the Pleroma.'

Replacing the codex on the shelf, Jack crouched down and examined a stack of thick dictionaries, encyclopedias, anthologies and grammars, at the end of which stood a row of slim miscellaneous volumes with faded bindings. He leaned forward to decipher the faded, tiny-lettered titles. Among them he spotted one that was familiar. So familiar it made his heart roll. He read, reread. He shook his head and rubbed the back of his neck with his hand, and read again. No, he was not mistaken. He was not seeing things. It really was there, tucked in between Pema Spielereine's other books. Toland's *Nazarenus*!

He took a step back to steady himself. What was *this* doing here? He plucked the volume from the shelf and held it in trembling hands. It had a different binding from his own copy and a slightly later publication date – 1720 – but apart from that it seemed the same. A facsimile edition seemingly. He opened the first page and a small card slipped out on which was inscribed a handwritten dedication.

St Gallen, October 1988
TO PEMA –
'My secret sister'
Staurogin Klaus

17

'I see you know Klaus.' Jack turned from the bookshelf towards Pema as she re-entered the room, the *Nazarenus* volume still open in his hands.

'Yes,' Pema replied. She halted just inside the doorway and held his gaze.

'What's Klaus's interest in Toland? Where did he get this?'

'Klaus studied him. We both have. There are some rare editions in the archive.'

'I don't believe this. Did Raphaëlle see Klaus here?'

'They often met at my seminars.'

'At the Klosterhof?'

'Yes, and at the Müller Hotel.'

'The seminars on Jung and Gnosticism?'

'Yes. Klaus didn't recognise Raphaëlle at first, but she instantly remembered him from her visit here with you.'

'And they've met since?'

'Of course. Klaus has been helping with her research on theological twins.'

'Thanks, Pema, but I've got to leave now. Perhaps Klaus will tell me where she is.' The words tumbled from his mouth.

Pema said nothing.

He collected his blackthorn and coat and moved towards the door. Pema stepped aside to let him pass. 'I wish you well, Jack,' she said. 'But be patient. Raphaëlle has her reasons.'

18

The sky was clear that afternoon, blue as a flame and streaked with trails, as Jack hobbled awkwardly from Pema's house. A restiveness surged inside him now as he waited for the bus. As if the walls of his world were caving in around him. He breathed awkwardly. He had got nowhere in his search for Raphaëlle and his dead brother was ghosting his every thought, thanks to Raphaëlle's obsession with doubles. And now this connection between Pema and Klaus – the dedication on the Toland edition – and the Klaus look-alike talking to Emilie's friend. It was all too much. One moment nothing connected, the next, everything. But none of it made sense.

He thumped his stick against the ground. What exactly did Pema mean when she said Raphaëlle had her reasons? What reasons? He began swallowing quickly, shallow mouthfuls of air until his heart beat fast against his ribs. There was a whiteness in his head. A shot or two, that's what he needed. But the bus wasn't coming. It was taking too long. He'd walk.

It was two kilometres back to the hotel. Small birds swerved about in the faint breeze. After a few minutes, he began to sweat slightly. He rubbed his forehead in the crook of his elbow and tried to work his leg movements into regular rhythm. He began singing something inside his head, to get some kind of beat going, but it didn't catch.

He felt sick. The meeting with Pema had brought back some moments he preferred to forget, especially moments in Columbanus Abbey after Sam's death when, dazed and numb, he had prayed with Anselm at Vespers. He feared returning to that place again. He feared the lure of the trance. The way he'd felt drawn to Pema just now as he'd been drawn to Anselm all those years ago. The calmness of the voice, the strong-featured face, the aroma of incense. He feared the way he had sat down without a word, the way he had taken the cup between his hands, between his lips, as in some priestly liturgy, the way he had breathed and chanted in his head and waited. But, above all, he feared the way his heart had pounded when he had read the gnostic codex and discovered Toland's text . . . Toland of all people! Yes, his whole being trembled at the thought of being drawn on to a path not of his choosing. A path on to which Raphaëlle herself, he now suspected, might have been drawn before him.

He had to know. He'd collect Emilie at the hotel and go to see Klaus.

Perhaps Toland's Spinozist theory was right after all, he thought, as he passed the last of the yellow poplars lining Gallusstrasse and turned left under the awning of the hotel. Maybe we do all live in a single determined space where nothing is an accident.

19

It was after 1 p.m. when Jack got back to the hotel. Emilie was out for lunch with Frau Müller and Margarita who had a half-day off from school on Thursdays. Herr Müller expected them back around three.

He went up to his room. He didn't like having to wait around before going to see Klaus, but he felt he couldn't be gone when Emilie got back, not after their exchange that morning. He could do with a cigarette in any case to take the edge off. It was four days now since his last joint and he knew the old withdrawal symptoms all too well, the nagging headaches and jitteriness, the fidgety moods and flushes. He lit up, and sucked deep, held his breath, then released a ring of white smoke. He opened the shutters and sat out on the narrow cast-iron loggia which was bathed in afternoon light. A day moon hung colourless in the pale sky, over the rooftops, giving off a liquid light. The air seemed thinner than usual. Spring was arriving after all, and every birch and poplar lining Gallusstrasse knew it, the tiny burgeoning leaves welcoming the warm breeze. He sat and smoked for a time, his eyes creased against the sun. He'd bought a packet of Gauloises on his walk back from Pema's. He loved the thick, tar-heavy smoke. He loved the way the first deep swallow hugged the bottom of his lungs and kicked his heartbeat into overdrive, the way it made his mind float. He watched the passers-by, mainly shoppers and pre-season tourists, milling through the stone arcades below, and wished that Raphaëlle was one of them. Then he looked down at the painted bars of the fenced balcony, his focus shortening, and thought about material things. Money and alcohol.

His credit account low after his flight over, he would have to watch every expense now. Worse, having finished his supply the night before, he had nothing to drink. Flutters of panic began to rise inside him. Queasiness. The shallow cough. He needed a shot badly.

He phoned down to the restaurant and ordered a large glass of their cheapest whisky – with lots of ice. He had that awful thirst that made the base of the throat raw. The dry scald. The thirst that only alcohol could quench. Cold alcohol, the colder the better, cold enough to make him gasp for breath when he took the first swallow, and feel the pungent perfumed smack at the back of his skull. Cold enough to make blood boil, to loosen knots, restore one's bearings. Chilled wine did the trick sometimes, or iced vodka, but best of all was Scotch on the rocks. More precious the instant held before the lips than breath itself. *Eau de vie. Water of life. Uisce beatha. Whisky.*

The drink arrived and Jack gave the service boy some change from his pocket. '*Sláinte!*' he said, raising his glass and toasting himself in the mirror. He swallowed hard. Steadier now, he laid out his Toland volumes in a row. He handled each bound copy meticulously, fondled them almost, one after another, his only precious possessions apart from his father's blackthorn and the Longines watch Raphaëlle had given him as a birthday gift. As always, he named the titles fastidiously, as if he were rehearsing the names of trees. *Anglia Libera, Vindicius Liberius, Adeisidaemon, Clidophorus, Hodegus, Hypatia, Mongoneutes, Amyntor, Nazarenus.* He clung especially to his volume of *Nazarenus* and wondered about the 1720 edition that Klaus had given to Pema. He was unable to comprehend how he'd never heard of it in all his years of research.

20

At 3.20 p.m. the phone rang. It was Müller at reception to say that the girls had returned from town. Jack heaved himself to his feet and went straight down to the lobby. He told Emilie they were going to the Klosterhof to meet a man who probably knew where Raphaëlle was. She was excited and begged him to let Margarita come too. She tugged at his jacket sleeve and looked up. He said yes.

Emilie and Margarita traipsed out of the lobby after him. Emilie flicked a hairclip in her hand, as her father expatiated on the Irish saints who had founded the abbey they were about to visit. She reminded him with a sigh that he'd already told her all about Gallus and Columbanus when they'd been to the Klosterhof on Monday. She rolled her eyes to heaven and took her friend's arm. Margarita put a hand to her mouth and laughed.

On the way from the Altstadt to the abbey, the two girls ran ahead and, out of earshot, sauntered along arm in arm, darting from one side of the pavement to the other, chatting in Schweizerdeutsch or French, Jack could not tell. He watched with a sense of quiet incomprehension, as if observing creatures from another planet. Emilie wore a purple shirt, her fourth change in two days, Margarita a yellow hairband and pullover. They both wore trainers and black stretch jeans.

He still couldn't get an angle on this generation. They

were streetwise, pragmatic, cautious, slightly indifferent, cool. Unlike his own baby-boom contemporaries who were always so recognisable by their single-minded idealism and flashy charm. Baby boomers were fed on demand and took their cue from heroes like John Lennon, Malcolm X and JFK – visionaries hell-bent on Utopia and heading for a fall. This new generation was different, initiated from the start into an already fallen world: AIDS and oil crises, ozone alarms and anonymity. Born disillusioned, they made sure they stayed that way.

He shuffled after Emilie and Margarita, staring up every so often to admire the abundant shops and houses decorated in neo-Renaissance and baroque styles. He had to move fast to keep up with the girls as they skittishly led him – Margarita showing them the short cuts – through a maze of narrow lanes, yards and passageways still extant after the extensive urban renewal at the beginning of the century. The two of them stopped only once to inspect something in a shop window before veering off again, shoulder to shoulder, in a fit of giggles. When Jack looked into the same window a few moments later he discovered it was an advertising gimmick for a sex show: a mechanical model of a monk standing in prayer, his robe rising every so often to reveal an altar boy in dubious devotion. He looked away brusquely, shocked to be so shocked.

Further down the street, the girls stopped at a pet shop and insisted on entering. Jack gave in reluctantly and hung about, ill at ease. Emilie and Margarita asked the owner endless questions about his different kinds of fish. By the time they'd finished he'd explained the origin, name and feeding habits of nearly every tropical species in his large aquarium. Blue and black Neons from the South Seas, Green Tiger Barbs and Whiptail Cats from Saragossa, multicoloured Platties from lakes in Australasia. He even fetched a catalogue at one stage in order to answer the girls' ever more elaborate queries. He read out the different names in German and English. And when Emilie, smiling over at Jack, asked for the original Latin names, the owner could recite them too. *Poecilia reticulata, Xiphophorus maculatus, Rineloricaria sallax.*

Emilie pleaded with Jack to buy her some guppies with zebra stripes and peacock tails. They were small, she pleaded, could be kept in a little plastic aquarium, and were by far the cheapest at only twelve Swiss francs.

Jack threw his hands in the air and said, 'That's all we need! A pair of shagging guppies!' Emilie, undeterred, persuaded Margarita to buy them instead. Margarita clapped her hands together and said it was a wonderful idea. They could go in with the Black Pacus in the reception foyer. No they couldn't, the pet shop owner pointed out, Pacus would eat guppies! Fine, replied Margarita, they could go beside them in a separate aquarium. She asked the owner if she could use the phone on the counter to make a quick call home. Jack watched as she charmed her father in rolling Schweizerdeutsch phrases, saying that a new aquarium would look *schönlich* in the lobby of the hotel and that she'd pay with her next pocket money. Emilie pressed her ear up to Margarita's so they could both hear Herr Müller's response. They each made a little jump when the receiver was replaced and marched out of the shop with three guppies in a small portable aquarium.

21

Once they'd reached the Klosterhof, Jack found his way to the archives without much bother. It had changed little since his last visit, except perhaps for the entrance to the famous scriptorium, which now had a plush service desk with enamelled lamps and a glass wall panel encasing the famous sibyl woodcarvings. But the archive vaults were still the same, built to the proportions of the original Carolingian design. A chinless young librarian at the desk informed Jack that Dr Klaus was out of the office for an hour. He expected him back after five. He mumbled his words, gazing dumbly through thick eyeglasses. Jack made an appointment for 5.15.

In the meantime, he suggested they all go and see the illustrated *Life of St Gallus* in the Oratory. Margarita muttered something about already having seen it lots of times on school outings, but Jack proceeded to lead them through the arched cloisters to the west wing. Inside the Gallus Oratory, he felt as if he were back on familiar terrain. He'd had no difficulty finding it, his mental map of the Klosterhof having endured remarkably well in the dozen years since his last visit. He ushered Emilie and Margarita towards the first painting in the *Life of St Gallus*, depicting a pious youth about to set sail from Bangor with Columbanus. Both girls met his exegesis of the scene with pouts of indifference. They were far more absorbed in their portable aquarium.

He then tried interesting them in the fanciful portrait of Gallus banishing wild beasts from the Valley of Steinach; but they whispered and poked each other as if he weren't speaking to them. The one picture the girls did react to was that of Fridiburga. Fridiburga, the beautiful daughter of the Duke of Constance, who sacrificed everything, her opulent surrounds, her future with Prince Sigisbert, her reign at court, to join St Gallus in monastic life.

And so, here was Jack explaining the same superabundant scene to his daughter which Raphaëlle had explained to him and Sam, detail by luxurious detail, all those years ago, standing in this same spot in the Oratory. The pale, unblemished Fridiburga, bedecked in scarlet velours tresses and purple tiara, kneeling seductively, eyes uplifted, before the bearded monk, court children and attendant ladies weeping coyly in a background gallery needled with sunlight. And the black-robed Gallus, poised and thin-mouthed, triumphal before his supplicant novice, knowing well that this alliance would cause a break with his lifelong brother, Columbanus. And not caring. The trance again, the lure of the trance which Jack feared, which Sam could never resist.

Emilie and Margarita stood facing this tableau, their eyes alert as those of young deer, taking in the extravagance of it all. For a moment, they almost seemed lost to themselves and to the fish in their aquarium.

It was Emilie who broke the spell. 'Why is there nothing here?' she asked, nodding towards an empty space in the sequence immediately after the Fridiburga picture. The gap in the series, the blank between Gallus receiving Fridiburga and his break with Columbanus. Like a vanishing point, or a blind spot behind the eye. Jack couldn't explain it now, any more than when he had first visited the Oratory with Raphaëlle and Sam. But he remembered the phrase Sam had used to describe it all those years ago in his diary. 'Pure space.'

'Why is there nothing?' Emilie repeated, tugging impatiently at his sleeve.

'I don't know,' he replied. 'I honestly don't know.'

22 $\int$

When they got back to the archive for the 5.15 appointment, the chinless assistant said that Klaus had been unavoidably delayed. He smiled weakly. Jack asked if he would be back some time that evening, but the assistant just stared at him from behind the counter. Jack then asked the girls if they wanted to stay on or go back to the hotel for supper. Margarita was adamant about returning, saying the fish needed to settle. She assured him she knew the way, only a five-minute bus ride on the route she took every week for music lessons. Emilie decided to go back with her when Jack said there was no way of knowing if Klaus would turn up that evening.

He saw them to the bus at the main entrance to the abbey and returned to the archive. He asked the assistant if there were any listings for J.J. Toland in the *Scottici Scripti*. He remembered the Latin name for the famous Irish Collection which Klaus and Anselm had shown him during his first visit. The assistant twitched his eyebrows, impressed, and agreed somewhat grudgingly to carry out a quick computer search. He turned up three entries on his monitor, printed them out and handed Jack the sheet without comment.

    – A 1726 edition of *A Critical History of the Celtic Religion and Learning, also containing the first Irish-Breton-Latin*

Dictionary and An Account of the Druids, Vaids and Bards of the Ancient Gauls, British, Irish and Scots. Otherwise titled *History of the Druids.*

– A 1697 second edition of *Christianity Not Mysterious.*

– A 1720 edition of *Nazarenus* containing a supplementary *Apology*, entitled 'Toland on Toland', preceding the constituent texts – *The History of the ancient Gospel of Barnabas and the Modern Gospel of the Mahometans attributed to the famous Apostle and A Summary of the Ancient Irish Christianity, and the Reality of the Culdees (An Order of Lay-Religious) as likewise The Relation of an Irish Manuscript of the Four Gospels.*

Jack frowned. This was the edition Klaus had given Pema in facsimile; but Toland's *Apology* was not in Jack's own earlier edition. He never knew it existed. He was certain, after his five years of exhaustive research, that, apart from this in-house entry before his eyes, there was no published record of this *Apology* anywhere. Incredible.

His head was on fire. He told the assistant he must see it immediately. The assistant drew back, recoiling from his zeal. It was on 'reserve', he replied, and could only be accessed with the official permission of the director. He removed a pair of tortoiseshell spectacles and placed them on the desk, as if to announce the end of the matter.

Jack insisted. He told the assistant about his previous visit with Anselm, an old friend of Klaus's ever since their novitiate days in the abbey in the sixties. He said he was sure that Klaus would be incensed to learn that he, a former personal acquaintance and doctoral scholar of Toland's work, was being denied access on account of some procedural rule. The assistant reluctantly relented. He opened the reserve room of the *Scottici Scripti*, located the 1720 edition of *Nazarenus* and showed Jack to a small desk at the far end of the room. Jack sat in the hushed space and opened the volume with trembling fingers.

This edition looked just like the earlier editions of *Nazarenus*, including his own – same red rubrics, same number of pages, same grey letters and lamp-ends engraved in copper rather than in wood, the only addition being the new *Apology* paginated in tiny Roman numerals and inscribed in Toland's own copperplate. Eleven beautifully handwritten sheets, entitled 'Point of View on My Work as Religious Author'.

But this one addition made a world of difference. So much so that he could scarcely take it in at first. Arched over the small pages, he kept reading and rereading the same opening paragraphs, his eyes washing over the letters, backwards and forwards, upwards and downwards, taking more notice of their visible shape than of their sense. Like a seasoned fisherman who hooks a coveted catch that has escaped his lines for years and hesitates, at the final moment, to land it with his gaff, afraid to end the hunt.

But Jack kept on reading until the words began to yield their life to him, little by little, syllable by syllable, sentence by sentence. He learned things about Toland he'd never even guessed at, things that made him shiver, things no scholar before him, it appeared, had ever come upon. As if, somehow, this unique and hitherto unremarked *Apology* had been waiting there for him to discover. He learned that the *Irish Manuscript of the Four Gospels*, transcribed in Armagh in 1138, had been passed on to Toland by a renegade priest called Jean Aymon who had befriended him in Amsterdam in 1709. Aymon, a devotee of gnostic sects, frequented the same circle of luminaries as Toland in the Dutch capital, a small group studying the writings of the second-century Gnostics from Alexandria. Accused by enemies of being a freemason and libertine, Aymon was obliged to flee Holland, but not before he had sold

Toland a copy of the ancient manuscript in question, a document outlining the heretical practices of the Culdees, an Irish lay sect from the seventh century condemned by Rome for its wayward teachings. Aymon had stolen the manuscript from one of the royal libraries in Paris where it was originally catalogued as a Latin manuscript with Anglo-Saxon glosses. Toland, a Gaelic speaker, immediately detected the error and deciphered the Old Irish script. He also ascertained that the text, *A Summary of Ancient Irish Christianity*, epitomised the unorthodox spirit of the Culdees, whose name came from *Céle Dé*, meaning 'one with God', analogous to gnostic cults of early Christianity. This accounted, Jack now realised, for Toland's enthusiasm for the gnostic idea of 'like-mindedness with God' and for Toland's remark that 'Rome errs, Jerusalem errs, Antiochia errs, the whole world errs; but the Irish alone are right!' It also explained Toland's sentiment, expressed in a gloss, that the world was indebted to the Irish for their 'secret learning'.

But there were more astounding things to come, things that shattered Jack's whole thesis that Toland was a rationalist dispelling mysteries, a scientific materialist determined to remove all mystique from religion. Toland actually described forming a secret society of brothers in the Hague in 1710, which must have been the first private lodge ever established in Continental Europe, and recorded the minutes of the inaugural meeting. The brotherhood was called The Knights of Jubilation and their meeting place the 'Gaillardin': a coffee house in the Dutch city where an élite of ostracised figures convened – Rosicrucians, libertines, masons, refugee alchemists from France, secret followers of the heretic Bruno, and printers from various clandestine Dutch guilds. Their 'goal': to pursue the secret gnosis and form a new religion. Their 'rule' in Toland's words: 'to be always merry, high-spirited, happy, ready to eat and drink, to sing and dance, to gamble and to joke, to frolic and play pranks'. Their motto: *bibamus, edamus, cras moriemur.* The meeting began with the following salutation to those seated for the 'pleasure feast': 'We, the Knights of Jubilation, to all those who will see these words: Greetings, Joy, Good Health! And also pidgeons, chickens and lots of fat pullets and capons and partridges, together with pheasants and woodcocks, cooked tongues and hams and deep-sea fish, *bonum vinum atque semper bonum apetitum!'*

He turned the volume round in his hand several times, holding it up to the light to verify that the *Apology* was indeed of the same stitching as the main 1720 binding. It was. He paused for a moment, then opened it again. Reading on, he quickly discovered that behind all Toland's ribaldry and jest lay a deadly serious purpose – the propagation of a New Commonwealth Religion with secret rituals and codes inspired by the ancient gnosis. Their insignia were the snake and the fish; their tutelary guides Minerva (goddess of science and printing) and Mercury (symbol of Hermes Trismegistus, mentor of Egyptian theology). Their basic message was that 'out of Egypt' and the Middle East came the three great impostors of monotheism – Moses, Jesus and Mohammed – and that 'out of Egypt' once again would come an occult knowledge to undo the triple lie, a totally 'unmentionable sect' for a new millennium, a new apocalypse, a new Utopia. The secret knowledge being that God was not only Man but also Matter. To this end, Toland informed his readers that in the same year as he had penned this 1720 preface, he had also published his last book, *Pantheisticon,* outlining the ceremonies of this new 'liturgy of knowledge'.

Jack squinted at the sentence beginning the next page. He reread it twice. Barnabas and Thomas were patrons of the New Religion. Barnabas because he was the most forgotten disciple; Thomas because he dared doubt the Risen Lord and put Knowledge – *prisca sapientia* – ahead of hearsay. Thomas exposed the empty tomb at the heart of the divine and revealed the mere carnality of Jesus. He thus became a figurehead for mystical philosophies of the late Renaissance, preaching one eternally moving cosmos, infinitely expanding through space in accord with the gnosis. Hence Toland's own claim, true to the vision of Thomas, that 'all the motions of Matter are but determinations of its general Action, for what's All in All Things is God, eternal and Immense'. An old gnostic doctrine which, Toland was convinced, would furnish the model for a covert Religion of Nature.

Jack's heart was racing so fast he had to pause for a minute. His shirt was wet and he could smell the pungent odour of his own sweat. He put his hands to his face and rubbed his eyes until they hurt. Here in these pages before him was evidence for Toland's most vicious detractors. The very things he, Jack, had been trying to defend his namesake against for years. Toland, it now transpired, *was* a double-dealer. Freemason and conspirer. Libertine immoralist. Gnostic mage of an 'unmentionable sect'.

He couldn't bear to take in what he was reading but he couldn't stop. He breathed in so rapidly it hurt the bottom of his lungs, and continued with the remainder of the *Apology*, balking at each new revelation. Toland, he learned, had been involved with secret sects as early as 1690, almost twenty years before he set up the Hague lodge. His initiation began in Edinburgh with a group of radical masons who believed that Europe had been saved from the Dark Ages by seeds of gnosis transmitted by Irish and Scots missionaries from the sixth century and after – Gallus and Columbanus, Sedulius and Kilianus, Marcellus and Eriugena the Pantheist, condemned for heresy, each bearing ciphered manuscripts to the courts of the Continent. And of all the famous archives founded by these missionary monks throughout Europe between 700 and 1200, Jack was sitting in the most illustrious of them all – the *Scottici Scripti* of St Gallen – and reading, more incredibly still, Toland's ultimate signing-off, his unpublished *Apologia pro sua vita*! The first modern text to attempt to restore the double God – the God of good *and* evil, the God spirit *and* matter, *theos* and *pantheos*.

The final shock came, however, in Toland's concluding dedication:

> *I end this confession of my hidden beliefs here in the scriptorium of St Gall, founded by my illustrious ancestor from Ulster, St Gallus, who found his way to this dark valley of Steinach over a thousand years ago. I dedicate this, my last Apology, to readers of the Coming Time and instruct that it be preserved meanwhile within the precincts of this room, guarded from a world not yet prepared to heed the Knowledge. Here let it remain, awaiting the Few who may appear in generations to come, no longer fearing to follow knowledge through to its end, the Few who may not shy from the great gnostic truth that the only way to divinity is to foresake it, that the only way to win God is to lose Him.*

Jack slammed his hand down on the page. Toland had been here! He had visited this same library three hundred years ago. He had met the monks of St Gall, strolled through these medieval arcades, perhaps even sat at this same desk. Yet no one had ever known. Numerous letters and accounts had recorded Toland's journeys to Leipzig, Dusseldorf, Prague and Vienna – even to Berne to visit the grave of Ludlow – but not one mention of St Gallen! Yet *this* was the place to which Toland had come to confess his gnostic heresies. *This* was where he had come to confide his unconscionable thoughts about God. Ghost begat ghost begetting. Doubling. The very place where Jack now found himself.

He suddenly wished Danièle were there. He wanted to phone her right away and tell her how wrong he'd been about Toland all these years. That she was right all along – Toland was a fraud. He looked at his watch. She'd be in class and he'd end up talking to her machine. But he would tell her. He owed her that.

23

Jack closed *Nazarenus* and stared blankly at the cover for several seconds before returning it to its shelf. The dark, elusive secret – coiled like an invisible worm at the heart of Toland's life – was uncoiling now before his eyes. Toland a Gnostic! Behind the enlightened rationalist a furtive mystagogue. Behind the scientist a sham. His double life a ploy of sheer duplicity. Five years of research in vain.

He walked from the reserve room to reception, hands jammed in his pockets. His pace was ragged; he'd left his stick at the entrance with his coat. He was afraid. The serendipity was now too serendipitous. The chance too chance-like to be chance. When he talked to Klaus he'd get to the bottom of it.

The assistant informed him he'd just received a message from Klaus. He'd left town on urgent business and wouldn't be back now for several days. Jack leaned heavily on the counter. He asked the librarian to repeat what he'd said. He did, each word, with the same brazen look. Jack lowered his face until it was level with his interlocutor, seated at the far side of the desk. He spoke in a spitting whisper, his features creased in fury. He said he couldn't wait around like this indefinitely, he had a daughter to look after, a wife to find.

'Not my business,' shrugged the assistant.

Jack cursed, slung on his duffel coat and made to leave. He felt ungainly in his great thick coat, limping along on one leg in search of his stick. Like Long John Silver, he thought, only he wished right now he had that fearsome seaman's power, the black spot, the force that sent Black Dog hunting after the lost secret in Black Hill Cove. His crutch a cutlass, his wit a brace of pistols, his tongue a fatal curse. He found his blackthorn where he had left it by the entrance and started to open the door. But something pulled him round before he slipped the latch, some needling air of subterfuge about the young assistant's manner, some suspicion he was hiding something. He hobbled back to the desk and banged his blackthorn on the polished counter. The assistant jerked back and grabbed his thick spectacles with both hands.

'Where's Klaus?' Jack hissed.

The assistant stared like a hare in headlights.

'Where's Klaus?' Jack repeated, this time raising his stick high over the desk. The assistant covered his head with his arms. Jack lowered his stick, pushed past reception, and headed for the director's office behind the desk.

24

'Remember me?' Jack stepped unannounced into Klaus's office. Although it was still daylight outside, the shutters were almost fully drawn. A large ceiling lamp illuminated the cramped room. There was a strong sweet scent of soap in the air.

Klaus hesitated, reclining his body in his swing-back chair. 'Of course, one of the Toland twins.'

'Jack Toland,' Jack corrected him with a glare.

Klaus tapped his fingertips together. 'How did you find me?'

'I threatened to skull that librarian of yours.'

'You must understand, Sam.'

'My name is Jack!'

'Of course, forgive me. I have many visitors here, scholars chasing up sources, looking for data, verifying some script or other.' He tidied some papers on his desk and clasped his hands. 'I cannot be available for everyone.'

'So your assistants lie.'

Klaus grinned. He'd aged all right, shrunk somewhat around the neck and shoulders. But the small, pale eyes were the same. 'So, what brings you here?' he asked in a smooth voice.

'I'm looking for Raphaëlle,' said Jack.

'I see.' Klaus raised a hand to his face and removed his

wire-rimmed glasses with a deft flick of his wrist. 'And you think I can help?'

'Pema Spielereine said you met at the seminars, that Raphaëlle was consulting you about her latest research.'

'Ah, you're doing a little therapy with Spielereine. Excellent.' A smirk played on his lips.

Jack took a step closer to the bureau. He didn't move to sit down and Klaus didn't offer him a seat. 'I came across the copy of *Nazarenus* you gave her.'

'Ah yes, the 1720 edition.' Klaus's eyes met Jack's then shifted away. 'A unique holding, one of my favourites.' He paused for a moment to inspect his clipped nails, then added: 'I recall Raphaëlle mentioning something of your interest in the Donegal mystic.'

'So you've seen her recently?'

'Recently?' A broad smile crossed Klaus's face.

'In the last few days?'

'She gave me a gift of this.' He revolved slowly in his chair and reached for a carving on the cluttered side table. 'Taiwo and Kehinde. The Yoruba double. You've heard of them, I take it?'

Two sculpted figures with plumed helmets and lozenge-shaped foreheads stood on a wooden plinth. Klaus passed it to Jack who seemed to weigh it, holding it out in front of him. He recognised it from Raphaëlle's folio. 'You're not answering me,' he said.

'Read the inscription,' said Klaus with a motion of his finger. 'There at the base.'

Jack threw him a furious look. Then, tilting the plinth, he read the carved letters, pronouncing each sentence aloud. 'When you meet your spirit twin you meet yourself. Twinship is a mirror. The gift of the twin is to reveal what in us goes unseen.'

'Interesting, no?' Klaus jerked his chin up. 'We're all after the same thing, aren't we?'

'I just want to find my wife.'

Klaus splayed his palms lazily on his waistcoat and leaned back, resting his double chin on his chest. He levelled a steely gaze at Jack.

Jack's face flushed with anger. 'Why won't you tell me where she is?'

'You've come to the wrong place.' Klaus replaced his half-moon spectacles, folded his arms and bent his head forward to resume his inspection of the papers in front of him. 'This conversation is over.'

Jack started to protest but stopped. He wasn't going to find out anything – where Raphaëlle was, what was going on, how Klaus knew about Toland. At the door he turned. 'Do you teach English at primary school?'

Klaus still did not look up from his desk. 'I'm the director of a prestigious national archive, not a schoolteacher,' he said.

Jack caught a bus at the Marktgasse and returned to the hotel. It was almost eight but, though he hadn't eaten since breakfast, he wasn't hungry.

∫

Emilie and Margarita lay on the bed. A video flickered from the screen. The two girls were counting beauty spots, freckles and moles on each other's arms as Jack entered the room. Emilie sat upright on the large down pillows and folded her arms. Margarita nestled her oval head against her friend's shoulder. They both wore mascara. Beside them, on the chest of drawers, stood the portable aquarium with the guppies swimming in single file.

'You know Dr Klaus, don't you?' Jack asked Margarita.

She shifted sideways in the bed, looking from him to Emilie.

'Why do you speak to Margarita like that, Papa?' Emilie dug her hands under her arms.

'I'm sorry, Margarita,' he said. 'But I've just spoken with Klaus and I think he knows where Emilie's mother is.'

Margarita's face puckered and collapsed. She looked like a gawky child.

'She's crying!' protested Emilie, removing the brace from her teeth.

Jack looked around the room helplessly. 'All I want to know is – was it Klaus you met today outside your school?'

Margarita's face was wet with tears now, her breathing ragged.

Jack sat on the side of the bed and placed a hand on her shoulder. He patted her awkwardly. His voice was gentle. 'What are you afraid of?'

'My parents mustn't know.' She said in Schweizerdeutsch.

'Know what?' said Jack.

'About the photographs.'

'Photographs?'

'I didn't do it. I never did the photos.' She gave a quick sob. 'I just brought messages from Klaus to other girls in class. But I never did the photographs. Klaus promised no one would know.'

'What photographs?'

'I can't tell you.'

'All right, then show them to me.'

She began to cry out loud. Emilie, looking frightened, took her hand.

'I gave them back to Klaus,' said Margarita without looking up.

'When?'

'This morning, outside school.'

'So why did you lie to me?'

'Klaus made us promise . . .'

'Promise what?' Jack had risen to his feet.

'To say nothing, never to show the photographs to anyone.'

Jack lowered his voice a little. 'Did you show them to Emilie?'

'No,' said Margarita. Jack looked to Emilie who returned his look, unblinking.

He turned back to Margarita then and waited for a moment before asking again, 'What's in these photos?'

Margarita sank her head into her hands and sobbed so hysterically that Emilie touched her father's arm. 'Papa,' she said, 'please don't ask her more questions.'

'All right, I won't,' Jack said. He asked Emilie to fetch Margarita a glass of water from the sink. Margarita took the tumbler in both hands and drank in large gulps, growing a little calmer with each swallow.

He asked Emilie again if it was true that she knew nothing, that she'd never met Klaus with Margarita. She nodded and Jack saw from her face that she was telling the truth.

'I'm taking you both downstairs now,' he said, ushering them gently from the room.

'Please don't tell my parents,' pleaded Margarita as she followed Emilie into the hallway.

'Don't worry,' he said, putting a hand on her head. 'I'll sort this out. Just go to your parents' flat with Emilie and I'll be back in an hour or two.'

'Where are you going, Papa?' asked Emilie as they descended the stairs.

'I'll be back soon,' he said. The two girls went to the Müller's as Jack phoned for a taxi. When it arrived he headed back to the Klosterhof. Stepping out by the abbey gates, he looked up at the rust-tinted sky above the roofs to the west and sucked the cool evening air into his lungs. He felt nauseous.

26

Blustery wind tossed the hair above Jack's ears as he hastened as fast as he could manage past the line of flickering yews at the entrance to the Borromeo Gate before proceeding through the arches of the Klosterhof's east wing. It was well past the official closing time but the archive was lit inside. He rang twice then knocked hard at the door of panelled oak. Nothing stirred. He knocked again. A bulb dimmed and flickered. He called out Klaus's name. There was no reply. He struck at the door hasp with his stick and the door gave way. He stepped inside.

There was no one at reception, no one in the library, Klaus's office was empty.

This was no time for compunction. He rifled through Klaus's files, sliding each shelf open brusquely, until he fell upon a catalogue marked *Confidential*. Ripped open, the file unleashed a flood of contact plates. They fanned out at Jack's feet like a deck of cards. What he saw brought a groan to his lips, as if he'd been winded. Prints of lurid, specular flesh, black-and-white shots of pubescent girls, exposing themselves, mouths half open, hands held up to heaven cupping pools of white liquid. A caption issuing from one of their lips: 'I offer you this gift, body of Christ'.

Bile rose in his throat. He pushed the photos away with his foot and wheeled round in a slow circle, not knowing what to do. Then, bending down, he plucked some prints from the floor and put them in his jacket. He rubbed his arms with his hands, then stood motionless for a moment, thinking. Moving to Klaus's side of the desk, he flicked through the phone pad, frantic now, almost tearing the pages out. He found Klaus's number at the residence and phoned. A concierge with a bored voice answered, saying Klaus was out for dinner. Jack asked where. His local restaurant, Schmithusens, she replied, on Moosbruggstrasse. Jack replaced the receiver. He sat in Klaus's chair and held his face between his hands, staring at the telephone. Then he reached out and pressed the replay button of the answering machine. A tiny green light flashed as the micro-tape began to revolve behind the glass cover. Jack listened. There was no sound at first, no voice, no message, just a faint crackle. He was about to press 'stop' when a thin, small melody began to play, rising slowly to a leisurely adagio of violins, cellos and trombones. Gounod's *Faust*.

27

Round tables filled the stucco-ceilinged space. Brocade curtains hung from high windows interspersed with paintings of portly cherubs. The Schmithusen restaurant was old-world, fashionably dowdy. Jack scoured each customer in the room but Klaus was not one of them. He was about to leave when he saw the young librarian walking from the gents'.

Jack grabbed his elbow. 'Where's Klaus?'

'Here,' a voice announced from above. Jack craned his head to see Klaus peering down at him from an upstairs balcony. 'Come and join me,' he said. With a discreet wave, he motioned his assistant to leave.

Jack climbed the stairs to the mezzanine and approached Klaus's table.

'Have some wine,' said Klaus, offering Jack a fluted bottle. 'My favourite Jurançon. French. From the Pau region.'

'I'm going to have you arrested!'

'Something to eat, then?' Klaus handed him a fold-out menu. 'The teal is gamey but excellent.'

Jack brushed the menu aside. He pulled the photographs from his pocket and flung them beside Klaus's plate.

Klaus inclined his head and scrutinised the prints. He balanced them delicately between his broad hands as if they were rare objects. 'Ah, so you've been through my private files,' he said, interrupting himself long enough to take a slow swallow from his crystal glass. 'That's larceny, you know . . .'

'How could you?' Jack cut in.

'I certainly didn't do it alone,' Klaus said, impassive. 'They agreed.'

'They're only children!' Jack's raised voice was attracting the notice of customers at a nearby table, but Klaus looked over and reassured them with a smile.

'If you really want to discuss this, I suggest you control yourself.' He gestured towards a vacant chair. 'Here, take a seat.'

'They're just kids,' Jack repeated.

'Children aren't innocent.' Klaus placed an open fist on the table, his fleshy fingers slightly curled. 'They're born with darkness in them. The darkness that's in all of us, Jack. The same lust to possess and be possessed. The same desire to fall.' He gazed at Jack through thick glasses. 'Remember Augustine's *Confessions* – the siblings wrestling at their mother's breast, eyes full of envy? A favourite text of your former wife, I believe . . .'

'What's Raphaëlle to do with this?'

'I've never forced anyone, you know.' Klaus removed his glasses, inspecting the lenses closely.

'I'll have you put away for this.' Jack, still standing, clutched the knob of his blackthorn.

'You misunderstand. I'm talking about theology . . .'

'And I'm talking about Raphaëlle. You know where she is, don't you?'

'Not so fast.' Klaus replaced his glasses and stared at Jack through the foggy lenses. 'Hear me out. I'll tell you about Raphaëlle in a moment.'

'So you do know.' Jack bumped against the edge of the table.

'We'll come to Raphaëlle, I assure you . . . after a little

Church history.' He poured Jack some wine. 'Now sit down.'

'Church history?' said Jack, angling himself into a chair with a jerk of his right leg.

'Yes. I presume Abbot Anselm taught you that at school?'

'Anselm?' Jack took a single, nervous sip from his glass.

'All those years at the abbey, did Anselm never speak of his obsession?' Klaus frowned.

'You mean his research into grammars?'

'I mean the Carpocratians.'

'*Carpocratians?*'

'Yes. A gnostic sect founded by Carpocrates of Alexandria,' explained Klaus. 'Early second century; he believed one should taste all human experience, even all vices, on the way to perfection.'

'That's perverse.'

'Of course – until you understand it.' Klaus dropped his bearded chin, then raised it again. 'Carpocrates believed that God is double. One side, he held, is full of light and logos – that's what Anselm and your brother Sam were after, the search for the perfect language.' He paused for a second to study the tips of his joined fingers. 'They were fascinated by ancient grammars like the *Priscian* – brought to this town on the backs of Irish monks a thousand years ago, fleeing Viking hordes as they followed the path of Gallus . . .'

'I know,' said Jack 'that's the reason we all came here twelve years ago.'

'Of course,' said Klaus. 'But there's another side to it, you see, the double God has a dark side too – the hole within divinity, the way of the fall, the way down into the pit.'

'Gnostic nonsense.' Jack's body stiffened.

'Oh no, it's in the Bible.' Klaus reclined in his chair and, focusing on some invisible spot on the wall, listed off some verses. 'The Lord has said He would dwell in thick darkness', I Kings 8. 'One abyss calls upon the other', Psalm 44. 'He redeems us from the curse of law', Galatians 3. 'Blessed is he who looks into the depths.' He gazed across at Jack, then added: 'Even God descended into hell, you know.'

'That doesn't mean he condoned evil.'

'He condoned the slaughter of innocents, didn't he? And the sacrifice of Isaac? And of Christ?'

'I've read the Gospels too, Klaus, and that's *not* it. 'I come to bring life and to bring it more abundantly,' John 10 – *that's* Christ's message. You're twisting everything.'

'I'm twisting nothing, Jack. I'm just following the first great Christian teachers – Gnostics like Carpocrates who knew that all was permitted once Christ set us free – absolutely free.'

A waiter approached the table and enquired if Jack would like to order anything. Jack declined and returned his attention to Klaus. 'I've never heard of your Carpocrates.'

'Of course you haven't, Jack. If Anselm never mentioned him to you, who would?' He spread his fingers wide on the table in front of him. 'Official Christendom couldn't stomach the liberties Christ preached. It censored the gnosis for millennia, condemned anyone who spoke its name. Augustine and Irenaeus were the worst inquisitors. But Christendom couldn't change Church history. The texts were there, the evidence.'

Jack narrowed his eyes and leaned forward. 'I don't believe Anselm was one of your . . . Carpocratians.'

'Oh, but he was.' Klaus grinned. 'We *both* were. Since 1963, our second novitiate year together here in St Gallen. I showed Anselm all the volumes in the library. Mandeans, Valentinians, Anchoritics, Naassenes, Cathars, Manichaeans – and, of course, the Carpocrations. He too was mesmerised as we devoured each of the gnostic gospels, scanned the thirteen tractates of the Nag Hammadi codices, read every single page of the Gospel of Thomas – the first Swiss edition was just published at the time by the editors of the *Codex Jung*. Utterly elated, we read more and more until we came to Carpocrates . . .'

'Who preached what?' Jack poked a side plate with the top of his cigarette pack.

'That the world is dual. The body corrupt, the spirit eternal. Christ mortal, the world a creation of angels.' Klaus sat back and sipped his wine. 'From which it's a short step to realising that the only salvation is excess. Asceticism or libertinism. Either extreme will do.'

'That's not what Anselm believed.' Jack jumped at the sound of a plate breaking somewhere downstairs in the restaurant.

'Oh yes it is.' Klaus proceeded unperturbed. 'Anselm and I were both convinced – the shortest way to God is through transgression. I chose one extreme, he the other, that's all. Anselm chose the way of purity, the ascetic way. He thought he'd find God through the lost language of perfection.' Klaus paused and, leaning back in his chair, placed both hands flat on his chest. 'He had your brother believing that too, didn't he?'

'Sam drowned.' Jack mumbled the words, his head slumped.

Klaus narrowed his eyes. 'Sam paid the price.'

'I paid too,' said Jack, still staring into his empty plate, speaking slowly as if caught in a trance. 'I lost my brother!'

'That's how it had to be, Jack. It was – inevitable. Sam drowned, you lost your leg. And Anselm left the abbey. Yes, your abbot told me all about it. He gave up everything that year – his cherished twin disciples, his monastery, his relentless quest for the gnosis. That's why he went to those famine missions, way out there on the Sudan border.'

'Sudan,' interjected Jack. 'Pema Spielereine went there too.'

'She did. But, unlike Anselm, she came back.' Klaus

smiled at him. 'You know, of course, that Pema is a friend of your wife.'

'Raphaëlle never had anything to do with this.'

Klaus raised an open palm. 'You thought the same about Anselm, didn't you?' He sat forward in his chair. 'Your abbot disappeared to the Nile, a monastery not far from Nag Hammadi, near Alexandria where Carpocrates was born. That's why you never heard from him again. Like all good Carpocratians, he kept the secret.' Klaus inspected the low wine level in his cut glass, then drained the last few drops. 'I was different. I chose the other way. I vowed that nothing human, no matter how fallen, would be foreign to me.'

'Including young girls?' interrupted Jack.

Klaus scrutinised the empty bottle of Jurançon then helped himself to a full-shot glass of schnapps from a carafe on the table. He offered some to Jack, who declined. 'Do you know what Carpocratians *do*?'

Jack did not reply.

'I'll tell you.' A light smile tripped over Klaus's lips. 'First,' he said, 'they make sure to keep things hidden.' He continued after a studied pause. 'They address each other with signs. Their favourite is from the Book of Thomas – 'Guard your brother like the pupil of your eye'. They use codes. *Reservatio mentalis*, they call it.' He moved his hand towards the candle on the table and pulled up his jacket sleeve, baring his wrist. 'They wear special marks on the backs of their ears and wrists. Miniature tattoos and insignia – a serpent's eye, a crowned Pisces. Like this.' He pointed to a spot above his watch strap. Jack made out the figure of a circled fish. Then Klaus did the same with his other hand, exposing a tiny tattoo of an eye. 'The serpent's eye that fascinates and liberates,' he intoned. 'The grace that cancels law – Law comes through Moses; grace through Christ.' He looked straight at Jack before continuing. 'That's why our Gospel of Thomas teaches that fasting gives rise to sin, praying to condemnation, alms-giving to the death of spirit. That's why it rejects the Jewish law against coveting your neighbour's wife and goods – they do not belong to your neighbour, they are not the property of one but all.'

'The innocent belong to nobody!'

Once more Klaus ignored him, fingering a clean plate and raising his thumb to his lips. 'The photos you saw? Love rites. Sperm cults based upon the Lord's supper, meticulously performed and confined to the elect.' Klaus paused long enough to see what effect his words were having. He watched Jack sitting opposite, shaking a bent head, avoiding his gaze. He stroked his clipped beard several times between finger and thumb. 'Men and women sat down to sumptuous meals of meat and wine. Love feasts they called them. Once they'd eaten, the women took the men's emission in their hands and offered it to heaven, then swallowed it, saying: "This is the body of Christ and this is the Passover; hence our bodies are given over to passion and compelled to confess the passion of Christ." Then the men took the menstrual blood of young women and said: "This is the blood of Christ; we retrieve our sisters' transgression. We collect the soul from all things and transmit it to the heavenly world." ' He almost hummed the incantations.

Jack lit a cigarette and sucked hard. He choked deep in his throat, repeatedly, as if he'd swallowed a fish-bone.

Klaus scrutinised Jack's face and waited for the coughing fit to end before resuming, still speaking with the distracted air of someone reciting phrases from a ritual. 'The climax of the rite was the bridal chamber. This involved spiritual betrothals in line with heavenly conjunctions. The liturgy culminated in physical consummation. Coupling openly with his partner, the leader of the rite endowed her with the Knowledge. That way he bestowed prophetic office on her fallen nature – through carnal ecstasy. Becoming one flesh, bride and bridegroom re-entered the One at last, the pleroma, lifting up the lost seed of light, returning to the origin. The cult was disseminated throughout Asia Minor and Rome by the first woman Carpocrates seduced into his sect. She was referred to as the "secret sister", the "primal twin".'

'It's an aberration.' Jack placed both hands on the table with a thump. 'You're using Christ to justify perversion.'

'It's not that simple.' Klaus waved a finger before Jack's face like a hypnotist. 'Not at all. Christianity is haunted by the gnostic ghost, believe me, from its very beginning to its very end. You can't escape it.' He lowered his hand and hunched forward, his voice descending to a whisper, as if confiding a secret. 'You should know that, Jack. No one escapes the dark double. The foil behind the mirror, the blind spot never seen. It's God's shadow I'm talking about, and it will not go away. Not now, not ever, I assure you, no matter how hard the Churches try, no matter how loudly tribunals and decrees and encyclicals condemn. Even the purest thinkers can't cast it from their minds. Irenaeus. Epiphanius. Augustine. Kierkegaard. Read chapter three of *The Concept of Dread* – the pious Dane conceding the Carpocratian notion of attaining perfection through sin. I'm not inventing this! They all denounced Carpocrates – but they couldn't hide their awe.' He tapped the edge of his plate, nudging it slowly to one side. 'Our friends, Anselm and Pema, were no different, Jack. They too colluded with the gnostic hunt. Even your Donegal namesake travelled all the way here to compose his last *Apology*.'

'They were all Gnostics?'

'Oh yes.'

Jack bowed his head and paused before looking up. 'But why? I don't understand.'

'Because the truth is irresistible.' Klaus fixed him with his steel-grey eyes. 'And every great mind eventually discovers that behind every science lies another science, a deeper science – *prisca scientia* – the hidden way of knowing.'

A flicker of uncertainty crossed Jack's face. 'Why would Toland go back to mystic Gnostics?'

'Because they kept the Knowledge.'

'But Toland never did those things.'

'No.' Klaus paused. 'He didn't have the courage. He didn't dare put his hands into flesh. He tried to keep them clean.' He raised his hands in the air. 'He wanted the Knowledge without paying the price, without going down to the hell-hole of existence. He saw the gnosis as a mere experiment, a search of the mind. Just like Anselm and Pema – and you, Jack, though you can't admit it.'

'Admit what?'

'That you're no different. That your hunt for Toland is the same hunt. That you've eaten the fruit and cannot rest until you feast upon the truth.'

'You're mad, Klaus!' Jack spat the words.

'I never mistake a brother.'

'You mistake everything!' Jack shook his head fiercely, pushing his hands down on the table to lever his body upwards. 'You're dangerous!'

Klaus caught his sleeve. 'I haven't finished.' He motioned Jack to sit down again, speaking with the steady voice of a conspirator. 'We were both postulants, you and I, monks *manqués*. We sought the same thing – to see the face of the God of Jacob. Anselm told me all about you, of course; he said you were one of us and quoted that Irish line about one black beetle knowing another . . .'

'*Aithníonn ciaróg ciaróg eile*.' Jack recited the words in spite of himself.

'Oh yes, your abbot had great hopes for you and Sam. Until Sam died.'

'It was an accident!'

'Of course it was.'

'Sam drowned by accident,' repeated Jack.

Klaus half smiled before adding: 'And your maiming, Jack? Was that an accident?'

'You're saying Anselm did it on purpose?' Jack reached for his blackthorn leaning by the chair. A fire was burning in his head.

Klaus didn't flinch. 'It's not about purpose, Jack. It's about God, God's own timing – synchronicity. You lost your leg the moment Anselm lost his disciple.'

A waiter came to remove the plates and asked if they'd like anything else – dessert, cheese, coffee. They both said no, and the waiter moved off. Jack waited for Klaus to continue. Instead he tipped his head back and leaned on the wooden armrest of his chair. He let his right elbow support him for a moment as he reached up and readjusted his glasses on the bridge of his nose. 'There's no point in talking any more of this,' he said eventually. 'Anselm was wrong. The Toland twins weren't up to it. Not Sam, not you. When it came to it, you fell by the way.' He pushed himself back from the table and cupped his fists on his knees. 'Mind you, Jack, when you visited me this afternoon and I saw your obsession, I thought for an instant, just one fleeting instant, that maybe there was a chance – that maybe your passion for hidden things, for Toland's enigmas and Raphaëlle's secrets, was special after all. But no, I see now you'll never be one of us.'

'So you agree we're *not* alike.'

'The difference between us, Jack, is that while you dabble I follow through. I make the knowledge flesh. *Veritas verbo et facto.*'

'You're perverting God!'

'No, Jack, just proving God is *all* things – good and evil.'

'So you admit evil?'

'Of course, as evil admits good.'

'Which makes it fine to seduce young girls?'

'Which makes it fine to let them be what they are – fallen creatures like you and me, as full of lust as the rest of us.'

'Remember Mark 9 – "anyone who is the downfall of one of these trusting little ones would be better thrown into the sea with a great millstone hung around his neck".' Jack stuttered the words, his face drained, his body tensed. He tried to push up from the hips, but there was still that awful weight in his legs, the drag downward and backward. He stayed sitting, transfixed by Klaus's colourless eyes, magnified into a Medusa glare by his glasses. 'What you're doing is abominable – it's criminal.'

'Of course it is,' retorted Klaus. 'And I'll tell you why: because our civilisation *says* it's criminal. But it was not always so, Jack. For centuries no one spoke of it, did they?—Church fathers? Augustine? Aquinas? No. And I'll tell you why. Because for them the greatest crime was idolatry – not believing in the one true God. For two thousand years *that* was the unforgivable sin, the sin against the spirit. But now we're facing a new millennium when the sea beast returns from the sea, as Apocalypse says. Everything is changing, Jack. God is dead, long live the child! Read your newspapers. What's the crime of crimes today? The violation of God? No! The violation of innocents.'

'And that's why you—'

'Yes.'

'To prove a point.'

'Yes. To prove that crime is relative. That we can be like gods if we dare.'

Jack lifted his right hand and curled it into a ball. His mouth opened and closed slowly, like one of Emilie's fish against the pane of the aquarium. Then he said: 'The Christ of love means nothing to you.'

'How could he?' replied Klaus. 'That Christ became a lie the day they buried his double, the day they hid his shadow in the empty tomb and the Church split humans into criminals and innocents, doers of good and doers of evil. The desert fathers laid the corpse, Augustine cut it at the joints, the rest is history, Church history – Inquisitions, crusades, holy wars, pogroms.' He poured himself another schnapps. 'Your Toland ancestor was lucky to escape. Make no mistake, Jack. What you call Christianity is a dirty business. Children of light parading around with haloes on their heads and flaming torches in pale little hands, chasing shadows, burning heretics, persecuting Gnostics in some mad devotion to purity and goodness.'

He drew in a long breath and held it in his lungs before exhaling. 'We Gnostics are different, Jack, braver, we're not afraid of the hole in God. We're not afraid to fall and be found out.' He leaned back in his chair, then pointed at his own chest. 'I too will be found out – and reviled – soon.'

Jack rose from his seat.

'As soon, in fact, as you return to your hotel to show the Müllers the photographs, and call the police.'

Jack was on his feet now, peering down at Klaus who seemed possessed by phrases beyond himself, his features intoxicated.

'It's the price to be paid for God's licence, for passing through all things on this earth, experiencing everything, so that when I depart I'm deficient in nothing.'

Jack placed the tip of his blackthorn on the table in front of Klaus's plate.

Klaus raised his brows and met Jack's stare. 'Degradation and hatred are what all Gnostics face. It's part of the test. I knew it would happen – and I welcome it.' He smiled. 'You see, Jack, I can't go any lower. I've been down to the bottom of the pit, a place where there's no light, no air, no law, where few believers dare to go. And that's where I discovered why God chose sinners over non-sinners, prodigal sons over righteous ones, why He wrote my name in the palm of His hand. Someone has to go down there, Jack, someone like me in every generation, to see the other face of God. The hidden face. The pitiless face. Unbegotten, cold, abominable.'

Jack removed his stick from the table and gripped it tightly. Glints of fury flashed in his eyes. He pointed at Klaus. 'And you brought others down with you?'

'Of course – that's my vocation.' Klaus placed his crystal glass carefully back on the table. 'I brought Margarita and her friends there.'

'You'd stop at nothing!' Jack clutched his blackthorn in both hands and raised it high over Klaus's head.

'Nothing,' said Klaus impassively, his head unbowed, oblivious to the staring waiters. 'But go ahead, do what you will. I'm not the one afraid – you are.'

Jack swallowed, his stick poised in mid-air. He couldn't strike. He lowered the blackthorn to the ground again, slowly. Lines of sweat formed in the furrows of his forehead. Klaus was right. He *was* full of fear. A terrible, clawing fear that broke inside him like a poisonous black fruit. Fear of what he'd just heard, fear of what he'd seen in Klaus's face, fear of how he too had followed double paths, his obsession with Toland's enigma an echo of the gnostic turn without his ever knowing it, his descent into the dark after Sam's death a lapse into another self, a demon so ensnared in self-hate that he forgot himself and his wife and daughter, and everything else that mattered to him. Yes, Jack feared these things, but more than all of these he feared the doubt – the cold unconscionable doubt that had flapped and circled like an insect in his soul ever since he sat down at this table, ever since he met Klaus earlier that day. He rubbed hard at the hair on his wrist. 'Is Raphaëlle involved in this?'

Klaus's features relaxed. He removed his glasses and stood up from the table, looking Jack straight in the face. 'You must ask her that yourself.'

'Then tell me where she is.'

Klaus reached over the table for the carafe and topped up his schnapps. His face darkened with brooding shadows like those in a Dutch interior painting. He drank, his neck stretched to drain the last drops, his Adam's apple bobbing as the glass emptied. Then he placed the glass beside his plate and said: 'Raphaëlle is in Paris.' He smiled again, the pupils of his eyes widening like blots of ink on absorbent paper. 'Forty-nine rue de Verneuil.'

28

Jack snatched the contact sheets and left the restaurant without looking back at Klaus. It was just past 9.30. He went straight to the central police bureau on Marktgasse and made a full statement, showing the detectives on duty the photographs he'd taken from Klaus's files and informing them where they could find the rest of the contact plates in his office. The police told Jack they'd been following Klaus's movements for some time, acting on tips from investigative journalists about a child pornography ring operating in the town. This was the evidence they'd been waiting for.

The police prepared a warrant for Klaus's arrest and asked Jack if he wished to accompany them back to the restaurant. Jack declined. His first priority, he explained, was to speak to Margarita Müller's parents and prepare for his journey to Paris the next morning. He left the Geneva address and number, in case they needed to contact him again. At the entrance to the police station he shook hands with the two municipal detectives assigned to the case before they sped off in their car. He stood there for a moment, in the busy street, looking left and right, not sure who he was expecting to see, his face drawn, his eyes bloodshot, his whole body dulled with exhaustion.

He walked the three blocks back to the Müller's hotel and showed one of the photographs to Margarita's parents. Frau Müller was inconsolable. She threw the prints face down on the hall table and collapsed on to the sofa, wringing her hands. She wept for several minutes and recalled how kind the family had always been to Dr Klaus over the years, each time he came to conduct his weekend seminars at the hotel, how they'd trusted him, how he'd always seemed so caring and concerned about Margarita, bringing her gifts and telling her stories. She wanted to wake Margarita there and then and talk to her about everything, but Herr Müller said that Margarita and Emilie were already sleeping soundly. There'd be time enough in the morning. They needed to think before they spoke to her.

29

In the early train to Paris, Emilie sat beside Jack, bright and intent, poring over a morning newspaper that Jack had bought at the St Gallen station. Jack touched the cusp of his mouth with his tongue. His lips were chapped from dehydration and lack of sleep. He lay back and dozed until Emilie woke him suddenly, poking at his elbow and pointing to an open page of the paper. 'Is that the Klaus you and Margarita know?' she asked.

Jack looked down to see a photo of a bearded man being escorted from a police van the previous night, a slight smile creasing his face, his chin jutting forward. 'That's him.' He nodded, staring at the figure in the black-and-white photograph.

Emilie translated the German caption slowly, her finger underlining each word. 'Klaus, director of national archive, held on . . .' Her forefinger on the last word, she looked up and asked, 'What's a *Sittenverstoss*?'

'Something you get arrested for.'

'I know, but what does it mean here?' She tapped the photo in front of her.

'Doing wrong things?'

'With Margarita?'

'Yes, and other friends of hers.'

'What sort of things?'

Jack did not reply.

'You mean the photos?'

Jack nodded, looking out of the window.

'That's all?'

'It's not certain yet.'

'Why won't you tell me? You're as bad as Margarita. She wouldn't tell me either, and she's only one year older than me.' She pointed again at the photo. 'Is Margarita in trouble?'

'No. This wasn't her fault.'

'What wasn't her fault?' she asked, leaning forward.

'There are some things I can't explain.'

'Like what?'

'It's complicated.'

'I don't care, I want to know.'

'I can't talk about it now.'

'When then? After we've met Maman?'

'Maybe.' He moved back in his seat.

Emilie hugged her arms tight and frowned. After a few moments, she looked up at Jack again. 'Do you really think we'll find Maman today?'

'I hope so.'

'Where's she staying?'

'In the centre of Paris, a place called rue de Verneuil.'

'What if she's not there?'

'I'm sure she'll be there.' Jack clasped both hands together on his lap.

'How did you get her address?'

He did not reply.

'Was it Klaus? When you spoke to him last night?'

'It doesn't matter. She'll be there, I'm sure she will.'

Emilie crinkled her forehead, looked away from the photo of the bearded man and pressed her face hard to the glass pane, staring out at the fields and trees and lakes speeding past, elusive, fleeting, coloured.

As he gazed across at her, Jack wished they both were somewhere else. Somewhere out there in the landscape in one of those green unpeopled forests full of hazel coppices and beech-woods where festoons of lichen and whortleberry would gather them into their sanctuary. Or far away, shaded by the cedars of Lebanon or the redwoods of Sierra or the ageless oak forests of Annamoe or Googanebarra. Anywhere he could protect her from his worst fears.

PART IV

She sat at her desk under high chandeliers and cradled her chin in her hands. Through the second-storey window she could see leaves recently sprouted on the trees outside – bronze, green, russet, yellow-white. A hedge sparrow danced along the branches of a poplar and seemed to sing but she could not hear its song through the double-glazing. The bird's mouth opened and closed, opened and closed, noiselessly. She unclipped a barrette at the back of her head and shook her long hair down over her shoulders. Inhaling deeply, she savoured the fragrance of acrylic resin from the sealed parchments stacked in the panelled wood casements on either side of her. Then leaning over the desk, she moved her pen slowly across the page in front of her, back and forth, completing the final commentary on her photo print. Dürer's *Thomas the Twin*.

Thomas the Twin puts his hand into the side of God. He touches the black gash. Since that moment the twin nature of the Messiah has been associated with Pisces: two fish swimming in opposite directions linked by a golden cord. The cord marks the line between self and other which leads back to the primal waters, the Source, ultimately dissolving in bliss or terror in accordance with the saying of Ecclesiasticus – 'All things go in pairs, one the twin of the other, for God leaves nothing incomplete'.

Augustine makes much of the Christ-Fish analogy. 'At the Banquet which you spread,' he writes, 'we eat the fish that was raised from the deep' (Confessions XIII). Augustine's claim is puzzling since in the same book he associates fish with evil and darkness. He talks of Adam's sons hiding from God's sight beneath a 'deep sea', embittered with non-belief and separated from their Maker by a great vault as they envelop themselves in watery flesh. And he tells of how God refused the heavenly food of trees to 'fish and whales and the great sea-beast' (the beast of the Apocalypse that will rise from the pit of the sea?). But if the fallen are 'sea-beasts dwelling in bitter waves', as Augustine says, why is Christ described as the Fish raised up from the depths? And why does Augustine use the Greek word for fish – IXTHUS – as an acrostic for Jesus the Saviour? Is he not suggesting that Christ is the beast of the sea, going down into the dark so that he might 'be in all things', descending to the pit of hell in order to rise up again? After the fall, resurrection? This is surely what Augustine means when he describes the Eucharist as a 'Fish raised from the depths and redeemed as food by the faithful earth'. But this Banquet is only for those who believe, says Augustine. So what of the doubting twin who disbelieves? Can he be admitted to the Banquet?

Is God one or is God two? This gnostic enigma, forced underground for centuries, survives in coded images that dare not speak their name. The Pisces image is one of the earliest of these, Dürer's image of Thomas one of the last. Through them the enigma lives on.

She sighed and reclined in her upholstered wooden chair. Was there an answer? The terracotta heads of the young women on either side of her desk – the veiled Zingarella and the open-lipped Niobe – seemed indifferent to her dilemma. As did the twenty-eight marble heads lining the L-shaped reading room with its twelve tables and one hundred and twenty-four chairs. She'd counted them all each time she walked around this Salle Gabriel Naudé, past the clocks and globes and ladders and latticed windows with their tasselled green brocades and the thousands and thousands of glossaries, dictionaries, maps and illustations filling its floor-to-ceiling shelves. The busts were mute now, every one. Senecca, Plato, Euripides, Demosthenes, Cicero, Marcus Aurelius, Daubetton. Not a whisper from one of them. Man or woman. Poet or sage. She was on her own.

She put the top of her pen to her forehead, then to her lips. She thought for several minutes, staring down at the Dürer reproduction in front of her, before leaning forward again and adding these sentences.

If God is double we are shadow selves. So argue the Gnostics against the God of the Jews, against the God of Augustine. But if God is himself, we are ourselves. Then Christ is Christ, Thomas is Thomas. Separate selves, not mirror-selves. One God, the other man. Is that what the black gash means, the cleft in Christ's side, the rent in his being – fission not fusion? The empty space in the hub of the wheel that makes the wheel revolve?

She replaced her pen on the desk and reached for a large sheet of blotting paper which she placed over the written page, pressing down hard with the base of her wrist. Double lives. She sat back and inhaled. Klaus's heresy.

PARIS

'As for tongues they will cease; as for knowledge it will come to an end.'

Corinthians I

∫

Jack and Emilie took the Métro from the Gare de Lyon to Châtelet where they had to switch lines. The electronic doors swooshed open and they stepped off the train. Jack walked close beside Emilie as they made their way through the crowded underground corridors of Châtelet-Les Halles to the number-one line, direction La Défense. They took this train two stations west to Palais Royal, then crossed the Pont Royal on foot. Once they'd reached the busy corner of rue du Bac, they consulted their pocket map and proceeded down that road until they came to rue de Verneuil. There they turned right on to the narrow street and found number 49 almost immediately. A five-storey building with a steeply pitched roof and small apartments on each floor connected by an open wooden stairwell in the courtyard. It was more modern-looking than the other buildings on the street, hardly a century old, Jack reckoned. They located the concierge, a kindly middle-aged woman with a Spanish accent, and asked where Raphaëlle Feher-Feldring lived.

The concierge led them up the polished stairs, adorned with hanging pots of white geraniums, to a *chambre de bonne* on the fifth floor. They knocked several times but there was no reply. Jack explained to the concierge that he was Raphaëlle's husband and that Emilie was their daughter; they'd come all the way from Switzerland to see her and would like to leave their bags in her room, if that was all right. The concierge nodded and, grappling with a batch of keys, unlocked the door and ushered them in.

'It's empty,' said Emilie as they stepped inside.

The room was scarcely larger than Jack's bedroom in Montreal. Apart from two chairs, a sink and a single bed, there was nothing. No suitcases, no cooking things, no carpets, no books, no papers, no pictures on the four stuccoed walls, not even a photo on the mantelpiece over the blocked fireplace. Jack screwed up his eyes and scanned the room for traces of Raphaëlle, some giveaway sign or signal. But there were none. Just bare undecorated space traversed by a single sliver of light, streaming in through the window and falling upon the chipped paintwork of the side wall. A lean reminder of the world outside, along with some stray muffled noises rising up from the street below.

'Aren't we ever going to find her?' asked Emilie, twisting a costume ring on her finger.

Jack turned to the concierge, still standing in the doorway observing them, and asked if she had any idea where Raphaëlle might be, or if she was coming back. She shrugged her round shoulders and suggested they come back later, indicating a place in the corner where they could leave their bags for a few hours. She locked the door after them and accompanied them back down to the entrance hall.

'What do we do now?' asked Emilie once they were back on the street.

'I don't know,' said Jack. They stood for a few moments looking about them, then crossed the road and headed towards the intersection. Neither of them spoke as they walked, gazing at the pavement in front of them with blank eyes. Jack knew that Emilie was crying. He could hear her sniffling even though she tried to hide her sobs by looking into the shop windows they passed along the way. He wanted to stop and turn to her, but he couldn't. He wanted to say something but he didn't know what to say any more. His leg dragged but that didn't bother him now. What bothered him was not knowing what to do, what to say, what to feel. He took his hands from his pockets and unclenched his fists, stretching his fingers out. 'It'll be OK,' he said. As he spoke, something touched his left hand and held it open, held it tight, pressing his fingers into a bunch. He looked down. Emilie had taken his hand.

They walked on like that for several seconds until they reached the intersection of the rue du Bac. It was then, as they looked left and right before crossing the street, that Emilie tugged suddenly at Jack's sleeve. 'There's Maman!'

Jack's heart leapt against his ribs, his eyes searching in all directions.

'Look! See! Over there!' She pointed to a boulangerie at the far corner of the busy junction.

Jack followed the direction of her arm and there, on the pavement opposite, through a blur of one-way traffic, he saw Raphaëlle getting into a taxi. Her hair was cropped short and died black but it was her all right. He called out her name, his voice rising from his lungs into the air only to be drowned by the roar of motors. Her taxi moved away from the kerb and was quickly swallowed in the flux of cars.

Jack and Emilie had to wait for a break in traffic before crossing the road and hailing a cab. His breathing ragged, Jack instructed the driver to follow Raphaëlle. Thanks to luck with the lights on the Pont du Carousel, they managed to keep her taxi in sight. There were just three cars between them as they crossed the river and swung out on to the Quai du Louvre, then tailed Raphaëlle's cab all the way up boulevard Sébastopol. They turned sharply into rue Blondel, a little street tucked away on the left, in time to see Raphaëlle disappear through a door at the far end of the pavement. Their cab was scarcely fifty yards from her now but was held up by a delivery van reversing from an exit. Jack and Emilie readied themselves to hurry from the taxi, but Jack couldn't find the right change, and when he did, he stumbled frantically on to the kerb, almost colliding with a lady coming in the opposite direction. Emilie grabbed her father by the cuff of his coat and steadied him.

When they reached the door, which looked like a side entrance, Jack rang several times before anyone appeared. There was a plaque on the door, *Chez Isabelle – Bar Cabaret*. A man with wide shoulders and a dish-shaped face answered. He didn't know anyone called Raphaëlle Feldring, he said in response to their query. A dim light bulb shone behind him. He was about to close the door again when Jack showed a fifty-franc note. The man stepped back and motioned him in with a flick of his head, saying that the girl would have to wait outside. Jack explained that Emilie was his daughter. The man insisted. They were the rules.

Jack took Emilie to a nearby brasserie on rue de Tracy where he spoke with the head waiter, installed her at a table and ordered supper. She protested with a little stamp of the feet but he insisted. He'd be back soon with news of Raphaëlle, he promised. He left her picking broodily at a *glace à trois parfums* in front of a TV serial playing above the bar, a story about a pretty girl caught between two pretty boys, *Helène et les garçons*.

2

The janitor of the cabaret let Jack slip past him on his return, motioning him downstairs with a nod. At the foot of the steps he entered a room through parted curtains, a long, low-ceilinged saloon bar lit only by occasional green and purple bulbs. There was a smell of stale beer and smoke. The narrow entrance and the sheer stairwell down into the underground chamber, the dimmed lights and dank air, all reminded him of the icon chapel in Columbanus Abbey where he'd prayed after Sam's death. But there was no gold iconostasis here to fill the emptiness, no painted angels with scooped cheeks and folded wings to guide and gather his gaze. Adrift in this cavernous gloom, Jack could make out nothing at first. He stood at the foot of the curving flight of stairs and lit a cigarette. The room flickered into jagged light for an instant, briefly illuminating a figure seated by the bar. He moved towards it.

'Is it you, Raphaëlle?' he said *sotto voce*, reaching out to touch the person in front of him.

'Is it you, Raphaëlle?' the person responded slowly, but it was not Raphaëlle's voice. It was a low male voice imitating Jack with a staccato foreign accent.

'Who are you?' Jack asked.

'*Moi-même*,' said the voice, in French this time.

'Do you know Raphaëlle Feldring?'

The figure took a long swallow from a clinking glass, then said, '*Y-a beaucoup de femmes ici, surtout le soir.*'

Becoming more accustomed to the light, Jack began to make out other people in the room, scattered about at low tables, huddled together, silently sipping drinks or pulling at reefers. Like a twenties movie in grainy, mute motion. There were people coming and going too, he noticed, crossing the interior dimness from an entrance at the side of the room.

His eye trained on the doorway, Jack sat on a stool at the counter and ordered a double Scotch. He emptied his glass in two swallows and ordered another. As he raised the full-shot glass to his mouth for the second time, he heard a commotion behind him and turned around. Someone appeared through the sweet-smelling haze at the far end of the room, black microphone in hand. Jack felt the back of his neck stiffen. It was Raphaëlle.

He lurched forward but his leg gave way under him, sending the stool sliding back against the counter with a clatter. People at nearby tables looked around, then away again. Jack righted himself and stared at Raphaëlle across the half-lit smoky room. At this range he could see she hadn't changed much, except for her dyed hair and her expression, more sultry and dazed than when he had last seen her, a slight sunkenness harrowing the eyes and mouth. But she still had the same calm look, the same painterly hands and bold chin. But why was she standing there with a microphone in her hand, rehearsing a cabaret number in the middle of the afternoon?

She began to sing then in a low, crooning voice, a jazz number, in English. *It was a cold and wet December day/ When we touched down at JFK* . . .

'Raphaëlle!' Jack called her name through a knot in his throat.

She lowered the mike from her lips and blinked into the spots. With her other hand she drew on a cigarette, exhaling through her nose. '*Qui est là?*' she called back through a waft of filtered light.

'It's Jack.'

Hands tugged at his coat as the barman prepared to intervene, but Raphaëlle shouted from her stool: '*Ça va!*' Jack stared at her illuminated figure as she stepped from the cabaret space and walked directly up to him.

'What are you doing here, Raphaëlle?' he asked.

'I'm not Raphaëlle,' she said, standing only inches away from him. She held his puzzled gaze. 'I'm Hannah. Raphaëlle's no-good, low-life, devil twin.'

Jack's heart pounded. He peered into her eyes. 'What are you saying? It's me, Jack.' He continued staring at her, scrutinising every feature of this face he had not seen for five years. 'You know you don't have a sister.'

'Raphaëlle *does* have a sister,' she replied, pulling a bar stool towards her and sitting on it. 'It's me. Hannah the slut.'

Jack slammed his cigarette pack on the counter between them. 'Don't do this, Raphaëlle,' he said. 'Not to me.' He pulled his head back slightly, narrowing his eyes as if to focus better through the smoke-thick light. 'I know I ruined our marriage. But don't do this. Please don't do this.'

'Do what?' she said.

'Stop it,' Jack insisted. 'I've come all this way to find you.'

'Then you've come to the wrong place, hero boy.' She turned away from him towards the counter.

Jack took a cigarette but couldn't steady it enough to light it. He put it down again on the counter with his lighter and leaned across to her. 'You can change yourself as much as you like,' he said in a fierce whisper. 'You can dye your hair, alter your accent, leave your daughter, move cities, switch jobs, you can change every damn brain cell in that head of yours, but you can't fool me. I'm your husband.'

'I'm fooling no one.' She took Jack's cigarette from the counter, lit it with matches from her handbag and inhaled. Still composed, she added, blowing smoke from her mouth, 'And I don't have a husband. I just sing songs for raunchy men who like my Russian accent, who like my looks, my smell, my touch, who pay me . . .'

'Did our life together mean nothing, then? Our life in Cork, in Geneva . . .'

'I've never been to Geneva. I've never heard of Cork.'

'Emilie, our daughter?'

'Emilie's Raphaëlle's daughter. I'm Hannah. I don't believe in daughters.' She took the cigarette from her lips, and slowly examined the lipstick on the white filter. She ordered a gin fizz and balanced her bare elbows on the edge of the counter. Then she began to speak, in a low, toneless voice, as if she was speaking to herself.

Jack didn't move.

'My name is Hannah Markovsky. I was born in Odessa, a citizen of the Soviet republic of the Ukraine, in 1958. Just months after my birth, I was abandoned by my mother, who emigrated with my twin sister Raphaëlle to the West, and one year later by my father, who died in prison. The state had me admitted to an orphanage in Kiev where I remained for five years until I was adopted by a family of Ukraine farmers.' She spoke as though in a trance, staring all the while at the smouldering end of the cigarette suspended between her fingers.

Jack shook his head. 'You're making this up. It's Klaus, isn't it? You've become part of it.'

'Klaus? Who's Klaus?' she asked. 'Someone I fucked?'

Jack bent forward and stared again into the woman's made-up eyes for some sign that might betray her, some message from the real Raphaëlle behind this mask. But no sign came. 'My God, what has he done to you?'

This time Raphaëlle did not reply, did not look up from her cocktail. She hardly moved except to trace a vague line along her forehead with the tips of her painted fingernails.

Jack signalled to the barman for another round and lit a cigarette. 'I spoke to Klaus last night, in St Gallen. I know about the Carpocratians. He told me everything. But it's all over now. Klaus was arrested this morning . . .'

'Arrested?' Hannah took a long sip. 'If you want to arrest someone, arrest Mr Leon Markovsky, the foster father and sound Soviet citizen who put me through hell for half of my life while your sweet saint Raphaëlle was swimming in so much privilege she almost drowned!'

'Stop it, Raphaëlle, please, stop. It's not too late. Just come with me and tell the police what Klaus did. Tell them what he did to those girls in St Gallen—'

'I don't know anyone called Klaus,' she cut in. 'I told you, I don't know anywhere called St Gallen. And last, Mr Jack Toland, believe me, I don't know *you*.'

Jack released a mouthful of smoke. 'I can't take any more of this.' He stared into Raphaëlle's hazel eyes, which flickered like candles behind veils. 'Come back with me.' He took her free hand in his.

She left it there.

He looked down at their hands, surprised to find them still joined on the counter, his on top of hers. She was breathing deeply, not moving her body, not saying anything more for several seconds as she sat there, face bent, leaning slightly towards him.

'You really want me?' she said finally, head still bowed.

'Yes,' said Jack.

'Now?'

'Now, tomorrow, whenever you're ready.'

'Now,' she said.

'You'll really come back with me?'

'Yes.'

They rose from their stools, Jack putting his duffel coat over her bare shoulders.

'I must get my things,' she said.

'Of course,' said Jack.

'This way.' Her hand still in his, she led him through the door off the main room. Jack followed her down a narrow passageway like a catwalk or cloister with exits every few yards leading into obscure cells. He heard a moan behind one of the doors as they passed. At the end of the corridor, they entered a small dressing room, blue-tinted, low-ceilinged, with just enough space for a mirror, dressing table and clothes rack. But instead of putting on her jacket and scarf, she turned to Jack and started to remove his tie. She took him in her arms then and enfolded him. He smelled a perfume he didn't recognise and brushed her hair back and bent his head to the nape of her neck. He held his lips there for several seconds and inhaled the smell of her skin. Then his mouth moved towards her mouth and they kissed and Jack remembered all the times they'd kissed before and felt how much she'd changed in those five years and how good it was that he'd found her again.

It was when the kiss ended that she laughed. Drawing back, she laughed in a way that Jack had never heard before. A nervous, hysterical laugh that shook her glistening body and sent shudders through his heart. Fierce and triumphant, her throat and head thrown back. The cry of someone Jack had never known.

He reeled back and stared at the woman before him, half clad in this filter-lit room. 'You're *not* Raphaëlle.'

'I never said I was.'

'What's happening?' Jack pressed his fists against each side of his head as if to stop himself from falling. 'What's going on here?'

'You tell me, Mr Toland. All I know is someone knocked at my door last week saying she was my sister and I believed her – for one reason.' She raised her fingers to her eyes. 'Looking at that woman's face I was looking at myself.'

'You really *are* twins.' He leaned against the dressing table, clutching the top with both hands. 'It's true.'

'Like I told you.' Hannah took a scarf from a hanger and twisted it slowly about her neck.

'Why didn't Raphaëlle tell me?'

'Because she didn't know.'

'How did she find you?'

'Ask her yourself.' She reached for her coat and yanked it from the rack. 'Ask that good little wife of yours who's invading my life, telling me things I don't want to hear.' She turned her back to Jack, adjusting her coat in the dressing mirror. 'She'll tell you everything. She's great at telling everything. Especially the bit about the minute's difference.'

'What minute's difference?' Jack addressed her back as she continued to face the mirror, fastening one coat button after another with slow, twisting fingers.

'The minute between her birth and mine. One fuck of a minute. I was born first so I got the privilege of staying on in Russia to live in hell on a Ukraine farm. She, born second, got a life of bon bons and ballerina tights, art schools and cameras, Swiss banks and cuckoo clocks.' She fastened the top button of her coat but did not look around. She remained staring at her image in the mirror as she sniffed her wrist then spat on the glass. 'I can still smell it on my skin. The high, sweet, rancid smell of sweat and vodka breath, of animals and ammonia and damp, foul, rotting earth and scalding seed all over my body. The smell I can't wash away. The smell of my foster father. The smell my sister never had to smell . . .' She broke off and wheeled around. 'My long-lost sister, yes. The one who turns up on my doorstep after thirty years telling me how awful it is that she had everything and I had nothing, saying she wants to make everything right again, to take the harm out of all those years I spent selling my body to survive in Kiev, in London, and now here, and even saying – how sweet!—she wants to bring me back to Geneva. For what? To meet my mother!' Her words bristled with hatred. She trembled for a moment, creasing her eyes bitterly as she pushed her face up to Jack's. '*My* mother, my fucking mother, the woman who abandoned me at birth and fled with my angel-sister to the West.'

'Why do you blame Raphaëlle for that . . . ?'

'I'll blame her for anything I want, Jack.' She grabbed a hairbrush from the dressing table and gripped the handle, holding it before her like a weapon. 'I'll blame her for bursting into my life like this with stories of a life I never had.' She raised the brush and flung it at the mirror, smashing the glass into a hundred pieces. 'Do me a favour, Mr Toland,' she hissed. 'Take that Jew sister out of my life.'

Jack lifted his tie and coat from the table and folded them over his arm. 'Where is she?'

'The Mazarine library, Quai de Conti.'

He left the cabaret and went to collect Emilie at the café on rue de Tracy.

'You found her!' she exclaimed, slipping from her chair and rushing towards him.

'No. But I met someone who told me where she is.'

'Are we going there now?'

'Yes,' he said. He helped her on with her coat, which took a few seconds as she kept putting the wrong hand in the wrong sleeve. 'Calm down,' he said, putting his hand on her head. 'And look, you almost forgot your purse.' He reached down for the coloured bead purse she was about to leave behind on the table.

He settled up with the waiter, fumbling in his wallet for the right notes. His fingers were moist with nervousness. What awaited him at the Mazarine library? He felt like a last quick Scotch. He ordered it, counting out the exact change, then cancelled the order. This time he'd face things as they were.

They went out on to the street where they hailed a taxi and headed back towards the quays.

3 ∫

They entered the Bibliothèque Mazarine, passing through a row of Ionic colums that faced out on to the Pont des Arts, straddling the Quai Malaquais and the Quai de Conti. A squadron of stout pigeons sat, bored and grounded, on the stone ledge of the entrance. Jack showed his McGill library card to a lady receptionist on duty and explained that he and his daughter were there with an urgent message for his wife, Raphaëlle Feldring. The lady checked the visitors' register and said that Raphaëlle was in the rare prints section on the second floor, Salle Gabriel Naudé. She handed Jack an elaborate form to fill in and, as he did so, proceeded to deliver a mini-lecture to him and Emilie on the priceless holdings of late medieval and Renaissance parchments preserved beneath these capacious gilded domes – antique collections of prints, portraits and *estampes* as well as a million rare volumes, 180,000 of which spanned the sixteenth to the eighteenth centuries.

Jack was shaking, a mixture of nerves and withdrawal symptoms – almost five days now since his last joint. He handed the completed form back to the lady before she'd finished her speech and, taking Emilie's arm, climbed the winding stone stairway to the second floor. They found Raphaëlle, just as the lady said, in the prints section, bent over a desk of waxed oak facing a casement window. An aqueous light from the huge glass panes illuminated the volume spread open beside her, *La Calligraphie et l'Enluminure à l'école des anciens manuscrits*. On the desk directly in front of her was the Dürer woodcut of Thomas the Twin inserting his hand into the side of Jesus.

'Maman,' cried Emilie, running into the reading room ahead of Jack. Raphaëlle swung her head round and removed her reading glasses. She stood up and enveloped Emilie in her arms, her long hair falling over her daughter's head. They held each other tight, locked like that for several seconds, waving to and fro like dancers in slow motion. Then Raphaëlle lifted her face towards Jack. 'I asked you not to follow me.'

Jack stood several feet away. He opened his mouth to say something but said nothing. He loosened his tie and ran his hand over his crown several times. He felt Raphaëlle looking hard at him for a moment, then turning away. She wore a green barrette in her hair that matched her eyes. She hadn't changed. He fidgeted with his stick and glanced about him at the plaster and bronze busts whose mute stares made him even more uneasy. He felt gauche and uncomfortable in his clothes, as if he'd slept in them.

Gazing from one parent to another, as they stood there not speaking, Emilie intervened. She took Raphaëlle by the arm and suggested that they all go somewhere else. Raphaëlle nodded and put the books on to the collection trolley beside the desk, replacing the cards in the *fichier des usuels*. Then, slipping a linen jacket over her shoulders, she led the way back through marble corridors lit by circular windows, past the painting of *Les Bains du Bourbonnais* with jubilant little cherubs desporting in a blue pool, and out on to the street. She held Emilie's hand as Jack followed. The air was fragrant with lavender, Jack thought. Or maybe it was jasmine?

Emilie pointed up at the blue sky streaked with jet trails then looked down towards the glistening water of the Seine. 'Can we go closer to the river?' she asked, stroking the smooth sleeve of her mother's jacket.

Raphaëlle said she knew a place nearby and, turning right on the Quai de Conti, they walked, all three of them, towards the Pont Neuf until they came to Le Square du Vert Galant on L'Ile de la Cité. Raphaëlle chatted with Emilie in French about missing school and her piano lessons. Jack fell back a step to let them talk on their own. The evening light was greyish-blue as they descended the steep stone steps to a strip of garden. A triangle called a square. Not so Cartesian after all, the French, mused Jack, wondering why he was thinking something so irrelevant.

Emilie ran ahead into the garden, as Raphaëlle and Jack stepped under an umbrella-shaped willow about to blossom near the foot of the steps.

'Ah yes,' said Jack, 'the old *Caprea pendula*.' He spoke as if to himself, and Raphaëlle did not look around. Then, running his hand along the grid-iron fence by the grass, he began naming each of the trees they passed along the way. Chestnut, fir, sycamore, lilac, cherry, oak, lime, beech, poplar. Even, curiously, a young Coastal Redwood with delicate maidenhair fern leaves and white-green flowers climbing up its bark. *Quercus petraea. Sequoia sempervirens.*

Corydalis claviculata. Corydalis bulbosa. As he recited his litany, Raphaëlle glanced up towards the clear sky, shielding her eyes from the large white sun shimmering low in the evening air. She led the way along a gravelled path past a green *cabinet de garde* that looked more like a folly or gazebo, and explained to Emilie, who had returned and was walking just in front of her, how this garden had become a special place for her since she'd come to Paris the previous week. She'd stroll over here from the library every lunch-time. It was the spot where the islands of the city converged and where Jacques de Molay, Grand Master of the Templar Order, was put to the stake in 1314. Sometimes there was even a smell of the sea, she said, though it was miles away. She paused, tapped Emilie on the shoulder, and, raising her face into the air, breathed in deeply. Emilie did likewise. Jack watched.

What was the Templar Order? Emilie wanted to know. And why was there a smell of the sea in the middle of a city in the middle of a country? Was it true the river was at sea level? Raphaëlle did not reply and Emilie didn't seem to mind; she had switched her attention to the figure of a clochard curled up beneath a bush, a blanket pulled over his face, an empty bottle in his hand.

Raphaëlle paused by a painted wooden bench close to the water at the northern tip of the square. She sat down at one end. Jack stood by the other end of the bench and hesitated. Emilie cocked her head, looked from one to the other, then walked over to the navettes and barges tied to a jetty extending from the islet, casting a last quick glance over her shoulder at her parents.

Finally, Jack sat down close to Raphaëlle and they both stared into the churning grey-green water. The air pulsated about them and light traffic, passing along the quays on the right bank of the river, made a droning sound like insects. After a minute, Raphaëlle turned to look at Jack. 'Why did you bring Emilie?'

They both glanced over at Emilie who was now standing beside the hull of a barge moored at the edge of the islet, varnishing her fingernails with a little red bottle and brush.

'She begged me to let her come,' said Jack. 'She was crying.'

'Ah. She knows how to get her way.' Raphaëlle smiled, then shook her head. 'So how did you find me?'

'Defay gave me a copy of the Gemini book and mentioned St Gallen. I met Pema there, then Klaus, who told me you were here.'

Raphaëlle nodded. 'Klaus wrote me a letter for the Mazarine library when I told him I was coming here. I wouldn't have had access without it.' She looked over to the gold-rimmed tower on the left bank, crowned with a weather vane.

'He'll be put away, you know,' Jack cut in. His voice trembled.

'Who?' She turned abruptly. 'Who'll be put away?'

'Klaus, of course. The police are on to him.'

'For what?' She frowned.

Jack watched a cloud of bafflement scatter across her face. He wanted to believe she knew nothing. He thought of Klaus and Hannah. He still didn't feel certain of anything. He scrutinised her pale, smooth features and looked into her hazel-green eyes. Straightening up on the bench beside her, he told her everything he'd discovered since he had arrived in Europe six days ago, including the photographs in Klaus's files. He fixed his eyes on the river as he spoke, as if the glinting waves rushing by just yards in front of him could set the tempo for his words, distract him long enough to see him through to the end of his account. He spoke rapidly, hardly interrupting himself to breathe, not knowing how much Raphaëlle already knew, his sentences bumping into each other, the sequence of events sometimes askew, the hes and shes and wes confused; he had the sense that his words were escaping him, volatilising into the air around him.

Raphaëlle put her hands to her face. 'Is it possible?' she said after a pause, repeating the phrase several times like a mantra. 'Klaus was good to me. You've no idea. So kind to me during the seminars. So generous with my research. It was thanks to him I made the breakthrough with the Dürer print!' She turned to him. 'It's some mistake. Klaus couldn't have done those things.'

'He did,' said Jack, holding her distraught gaze. 'There was another side to him. A side that you and Pema never knew about. A side perhaps no one knew until he was found out.' He paused. 'You see, Klaus was a Carpocratian.'

'A what?' said Raphaëlle, wrinkling up her face.

Jack told her about Klaus's involvement in the gnostic cult, and Anselm's also.

Raphaëlle looked away as he spoke, staring up through the serrated leaves of the surrounding chestnut trees, still shaking her head as she rocked back and forth on the edge of her seat, her hands tucked tightly under her arms.

Jack thought how her rocking movements resembled the davoning motions of old rabbis at the Seder rituals they had attended together with Belle-Mère and Emilie each Passover they had spent in Geneva. He hesitated before adding: 'I even feared *you* were involved.'

'Me!' Raphaëlle swung her whole body round and glared at him. 'How could you! Don't you know me better than that? Is that why you followed me?'

'No,' he replied instantly. 'I followed you because I had to find you. I couldn't just wait around in Geneva not knowing what was happening. That's why I went to St Gallen, where I ran into Klaus, yesterday.'

'And he confessed?'

'Not before I found the photographs.'

'And you really thought *I* was involved?' She tapped her breastbone with her fist, making a light thumping sound.

'I was worried, that's all. I had to come.'

She took her linen jacket off and folded it on the back of the bench behind her, then turned back towards him 'I needed time alone here, to be with someone.'

'I know,' he interrupted, 'I've met Hannah.'

Raphaëlle put a hand to her mouth. 'What?'

'I thought she was you and followed her to the cabaret on rue Blondel this afternoon.' He placed his hand on the bench not far from Raphaëlle's. 'Why did you never tell me you had a twin?'

'Because I didn't know,' she replied, a catch in her throat, 'not until eight months ago.'

'So Hannah told the truth, then.' He shook his head. 'She said so many crazy things, I didn't know what to believe.'

Raphaëlle didn't look at him but fixed her gaze on a multicoloured slick of oil filming the surface of the water.

'Talk to me,' Jack said. 'Tell me what's true and not true.' He lit a cigarette and blew smoke out of the side of his mouth, waiting for her to speak, staring patiently as a low-gunnelled tug laden with cargo glided by just yards away.

After a few moments, Raphaëlle tilted her head and shoulders forward, her elbows resting on her knees. 'When I set out to find Hannah, I expected so much. I thought I'd find someone who'd explain everything, who'd fill in the missing pieces in my life, help me understand why I got involved with twin brothers, married one and watched the other buried. Someone who'd listen to the story of my life and tell me about hers – the life I might have had had I been the one to stay behind in Russia. Before I actually found her here in Paris, I fantasised about Hannah as a perfect soulmate, someone out there with the same skin, the same favourite colours, the same dreams, someone who'd understand me better than I understood myself. Who'd reveal me to myself. Who'd fill the gaps in my life.' She paused and fumbled in her bag for a handkerchief. 'But that's not what I found.'

'She was furious with you when we spoke today,' said Jack. He patted his pockets for a tissue but found nothing. 'I'm sorry things haven't worked out.'

'She was angry with me from the day we met.'

'Here in Paris?'

'Yes, last week.'

'Because you were chosen over her when you were born?'

'It's not as simple as that.' She shook her head.

'Is it true she was sent to an orphanage in Russia while you emigrated with your mother to the West?'

'Yes.'

'But how could that happen?' Jack removed a piece of tobacco from his tongue.

'I'll tell you from the beginning, like I told Hannah.' She pushed a pebble with the toe of her boot and hesitated for a few seconds before continuing. 'I came home from work one night last September to find Mother crying in the hallway. You know she never cries. I asked her what was wrong but she couldn't speak. She just kept pointing to a letter lying there open on the hall table, a letter with a Soviet address.' She paused, clasping her hands together on her lap. 'Mother was shaking so badly I had to take her in my arms to calm her, like I used to calm Emilie when she'd wake with nightmares as an infant. Remember? It took her a long while to speak, but she did eventually, and when she did, sitting there on the hall chair staring at the open letter in her hand, she told me everything.'

Jack nodded for her to continue.

'First, she told me how she'd given birth to twins and been separated from one of them . . .'

'How could your mother allow it?'

'She had no choice. She did everything to keep us both but the authorities refused.'

'What authorities?'

'Listen, Jack. It's not easy to tell this.'

He sat back. 'I'm sorry. Go on.'

'My parents were Jews. You know that. What you don't know is that they were both leading militants in the refusnik movement in the Ukraine in the fifties. It was at the height of the Cold War and the Stalinists were coming down hard on dissidents. When my mother discovered she was pregnant, my parents decided to emigrate. They'd already been subject to repeated harassment and knew it was time to leave. They applied for visas but were refused; so they tried leaving the country illegally, crossing over the Czech border. They were caught and detained. Mother gave birth in a prison hospital near Lvov, a long labour followed by a breach birth under anaesthetic. When she awoke the doctors were standing over her with two infants in their arms. Two girls. Twins. Identical. Me and Hannah.'

'Was your father there?'

'He was in the same detention centre, awaiting trial with Mother, but he wasn't permitted any contact with us.'

'So how did you and Hannah get separated?'

Raphaëlle inhaled deeply and looked up at a nearby bush where a waxwing was feeding on a crop of berries. She reached across and took Jack's stick. Holding it out like a diviner's switch, she pinpointed a spot on the ground directly in front of her and jabbed at it. She leaned forward and resumed, a flutter in her breath.

'The Stalinists decided to make an example of my parents. They were very anti-Semitic in the Ukraine at the time and accused Mother and Father of being part of an international network bent on undermining national Soviet security. They staged a tribunal in the detention centre where they decreed that Mother was to be deported to the West, while Father was detained in prison pending future release on good behaviour . . .'

'And you and Hannah?'

'The tribunal eventually settled on a Solomonic carve-up. One of us could leave with Mother, they said, the other was to remain in Father's custody for the time being. Both my parents protested; they pleaded and pleaded but the authorities were unbending. Mother refused to choose, so the tribunal chose for her.'

She broke off and stared down at the Seine, furling and unfurling in an eddy of wash as it powered through the arch of the Pont Neuf. Her shoulders dropped. 'Since the hospital files recorded that Hannah was born one minute before me, she was granted the right to remain a Soviet citizen under our father's care. Since I was born second, I was given the status of deportee. That was 12 May 1959, the day our future was decided by a hair's breadth. A single minute made all the difference. I could have had her life, Jack. And she could have had mine. Our fate determined by one minute's difference.'

She folded one hand over the other, rubbing them slowly together as if grinding some invisible nugget of hurt. 'Mother and I arrived first in Prague and shortly afterwards travelled to Geneva. Father's appeal was repeatedly deferred; he was kept in detention in Odessa where he died of a heart attack before the year was out. When Mother received the news she immediately applied for a return visa in order to bury Father and regain custody of Hannah. But she was refused. She spent months and months travelling to and from the Soviet embassy in Bern, filling out new application forms. Each time the visa was turned down; and Mother received no official news of Hannah's whereabouts for months until one day in the winter of 1960 she was notified that Hannah had been adopted by a Ukrainian family and was happily settled. No further information could be given, in response to her enquiries, owing to the strict adoption laws of the time. Nobody could help. Mother suffered a breakdown, was hospitalised for several weeks, and once she got out never spoke of Hannah again.'

'And you never knew?' Jack frowned at her.

'No. Not until the letter arrived eight months ago. She never told me.'

'But why?'

Raphaëlle let out a small sigh. 'I've tried to understand. She says she didn't want me growing up suffering as she had – always thinking about Hannah. She didn't want me spending my life wondering what had become of her, my missing twin somewhere out there in the world, left behind.' She covered her face with her hands and wept quietly.

Jack moved a hand towards her, but pulled away. 'Why did it take so long to find her? You said you got the letter eight months ago.'

She took a long breath and sat up straight, not looking at him. 'It took that long to get the records from the Soviet government, even with all this talk of glasnost. Maybe because it's such a sensitive case. The Bern embassy spent seven months trying to trace Hannah's emigration papers before finally coming up with her address two weeks ago – which is when I wrote to you and came straight here to Paris.'

She clenched her hands into fists. 'It was so awful these past months, knowing she existed but not knowing where she was – or even if she was alive.' Her long hair fell down over her face, covering her green eyes. 'Now I've found her and she hates me. And I can't blame her.'

'You can't blame yourself, surely.'

'Maybe not, but the guilt doesn't go away.'

'Guilt?'

'You know, Jack – the guilt of the survivor.'

Jack stared down at his hands, curling his palms open as if the criss-crossing lines on that landscape of skin might offer some answer. 'You're right. I do know. And look what it did for me.'

Still not looking at him, Raphaëlle said, 'Believe me, Jack, I understand that now in a way I never did before.' Her voice was low but firm. 'I've thought about you all the time these past months. Every day as I waited and waited for news of Hannah's whereabouts. That's when I started the work on Gemini, reproducing all those images and prints, visiting Pema. It got to the point where I couldn't actually think about me and Hannah without thinking about you and Sam. As if your story was ghosting mine. As if I'd suddenly got inside your mind in a way I never could when we were together.' She glanced at him, sitting there beside her, head bowed, still inspecting the lines on his palms. 'I suddenly knew why you could never get over Sam's loss. Why you blamed yourself.'

She raised a hand to one ear and twisted a small pearl earring between her fingers. It was an old reflex of hers whenever she was confused, and the recognition of it made Jack's heart swing open. He bit his lip and looked up, squinting hard into the sunlight shimmering off the edges of the river.

'And I vowed, Jack, that with Hannah and me it would be different. I'd find her whatever it took. And I'd make it up to her.'

He raised his head and took a long breath. 'But it didn't turn out that way.'

'No, it didn't.' She shrugged her shoulders. 'Nothing turned out like it should have. Hannah didn't want to hear any of this, as you know. But still I had to tell her. It's not just my story; it's *our* story, hers and mine. And it doesn't make sense without her.'

Jack nodded.

'I didn't expect her to be that angry. I just wasn't prepared for hate. From the moment I showed up last week on her doorstep, from the moment she opened the door, Hannah didn't want to know me. She stood there paralysed at first, as if she was in the middle of a nightmare and needed to pinch herself to see if it was real. She looked me up and down, standing there in her hall, as though she was inspecting herself in new clothes in an outfitter's mirror.'

'Did she talk to you?'

'Very little that first time. She kept asking me how I found out that she existed, how I'd discovered we were twins.'

'She knew nothing either?'

'Nothing. Until I told her what Mother told me last September. How both our parents were initially convinced that the Ukrainian court would relent within weeks and let Hannah join Mother and me in the West. How Mother had written again and again and Father had petitioned the prison officials in Lvov every day for over a year, saying it wasn't natural to separate a mother from one of her twins like that, until the repeated refusal of the authorities crushed his spirit and his heart. And I explained as best I could to Hannah how the court, after Father's death, had sent her to a state home for adoption—'

'—which is when Hannah's real horror story began.'

'Yes. But we didn't get that far the first day. As soon as I mentioned the adoption, she said she didn't want to talk any more.'

'But you met again.'

'We did. I had to phone her several times to persuade her. The first two times she hung up, but the third time she let me talk for a bit. She didn't say anything and refused to let me speak another word about Mother and Father, but she did let me tell her a little about my marrying a twin, and the break-up and Emilie. And after a few more calls, she started to ask me some questions about what it had been like living with a man whose twin had died and who had only one leg and serious addictions. And I told her, and I didn't spare the details, including the last night when Emilie found you on the floor and became hysterical, thinking you were dead . . .'

'You told her everything?'

'Yes, and we met a few times after that in a little room I rented.'

'Emilie and I went there this morning, Klaus gave us the address – it's completely bare. We were afraid you'd moved out.'

Raphaëlle was silent for a moment before continuing. 'I wanted it like that. A space with nothing of me in it. And nothing of her. Like a vacant lair. I suppose I was thinking of an empty womb, I don't know, somewhere we could start over, as if from the beginning, telling each other's stories, exchanging memories and dreams we might have shared had we grown up together.'

She brushed away a swarm of small flies forming a dizzy halo above her head, ducking slightly as she waved her hand in the air. 'Our stories were just too different. She told me today she hates the fact we look the same – but aren't the same. She hates the very fact that I exist. She doesn't want to see me again.' Raphaëlle touched her cheekbones, then turned towards him. 'I thought I'd find my other half in Hannah, but what I found was someone more different from me than anyone I've ever met.'

'Will you tell Emilie about Hannah?' Jack looked over at Emilie sitting cross-legged by stone steps leading down to the barges, enjoying the evening sun.

'Of course.'

'Do you think Hannah will agree to meet her?'

'No. Not yet. But I haven't given up. She's still too angry. It's only been a week, she hasn't had time to take in what's happening. I've had eight months – and look what it did to me! I abandoned everything until I found her. Her reaction is no more extreme; just opposite. But then, we had opposite lives, didn't we?' She fell silent and gazed down at some shiny twigs bobbing about in the water below. 'I'll wait for a while before trying to see her again.'

'You think she'll come around?'

'I have to try. She's my lost sister – now that I've found her I can't give her up.'

'Did she give you any reason to hope?'

Raphaëlle nodded. 'During one of our meetings this week, I happened to mention I hadn't said anything to Emilie about all this. At that, Hannah turned her face towards the window to hide the fact that she was upset, then kept repeating: "You must tell her, you must tell her!" And when I asked why she said because that's what happened to her and me: we were *never* told. She grabbed me tightly by the arms until I promised I would tell Emilie.' Raphaëlle paused. 'It was the only time Hannah touched me.'

Jack looked at her as she stared into the mottled waves flowing through the Pont des Arts. He wanted to lean across and enfold her soft-boned body in his, to kiss her neck and hair and forehead, to wipe the grief away from her eyes. But he didn't.

She removed her beige linen jacket from the back of the bench and pulled it tight about her shoulders, though the air was not cold. 'How's your leg?' She asked after a while. She spoke a little more easily now, almost like a neighbour commenting on the weather.

'One is fine and the other doesn't know the difference.' He uttered a short laugh and prodded his feet, one after the other, with his blackthorn.

'And Montreal?'

He sighed but didn't answer at first. Instead he lifted the tip of his stick and pointed to a streak of coloured wrack spreading out on the water beneath like a rough map of the world. Then, placing his stick down on the bench, he told Raphaëlle how he'd managed to get off heavy drugs and temper his drinking – he was shaky still but clean – and how he'd spent five years researching J.J. Toland, the Donegal scientist he and Sam first learned about from Anselm, the namesake who, she'd remember, had obsessed him even in Geneva and then all these years at McGill, until he'd discovered – the previous day in St Gallen – that he wasn't a rationalist at all, but the very opposite: a secret Gnostic. Yes, even his Irish namesake had turned out to be a double! Toland wasn't the man Jack had thought he was. He hiked his shoulders back and flicked the butt of his cigarette into the stained, dappled water.

'You're giving up the ghost, then?' she asked.

'I've been fooled long enough,' he shrugged. 'Five years on a false trail. I never doubted Toland, I never doubted Anselm – and now I find they were both frauds.' He looked at her as she bent over and picked a pebble from the ground, held it in the hollow of her hand for an instant, then tossed it into the water. The piece of gravel made a tiny plop, sending eddies rippling out from a pinprick in the water.

'You still haven't told me exactly why you followed me here,' she said.

'It was the folder Defay gave me. All those images of twins. I thought it had something to do with me and Sam.'

She raised her brows and waited for him to continue.

'I thought it might have something to do with Sam being Emilie's father . . .'

She rose briskly from the bench and shook her head. 'How many times have I told you, Jack – Sam is not Emilie's father.'

'But how can you be sure?' He remained sitting, his eyes peering down at the gravel.

'Because I never slept with Sam.' She breathed in and out rapidly. 'I've told you. I met him because he asked me to come. He was upset. That's when he confessed his desire for me, his confusion about his calling. I tried to help but I couldn't. I've had to live with that. I loved him too. But I didn't sleep with him the night he drowned, nor any other night. You could never believe me.'

Jack kept his head bowed.

'Just look at you sitting there. After all this time, you're still locked up in your jealousy and doubt.' She walked several paces towards the river, plucking a leaf from a hanging chestnut branch. Congested traffic crawled past the bookstalls and poplars on the Quai Malaquais opposite. She peeled the pale-green leaf along its capillary lines towards the stem and clenched it in her fist. She turned back to him then, her voice trembling. 'That's what destroyed everything, Jack. Your doubting me.'

He shifted on the bench and looked straight at Raphaëlle as she stood by the water's edge. 'It's true. I had to doubt. You were right. I needed the uncertainty, the envy. I *had* to be betrayed.'

She held his gaze, wrinkles creasing the edges of her eyes. 'That's the craziness of it. Sam wanted me, but he could never bear the thought of betraying you, even in his mind.'

Jack nodded slowly. 'I was wrong about Sam. I see that now.' He paused. 'I was wrong about you too.'

Raphaëlle turned away again. She watched a couple of early swallows dive and swivel through the evening air before adding, in a calmer voice. 'You never got over Sam. And you never will, Jack – any more than I'll get over Hannah. But we've also got to let them go, let them be themselves, not what we imagined them to be.' Raphaëlle faced Jack. 'If we can live with the gap they've left inside us, maybe we can live with each other.'

'You think so?'

'I do.'

'Is that why you called me back?'

She peered up at the sky before replying, shielding her eyes as she followed the swallows' flight down past the roofs of La Samaritaine. She raised her fingers to the base of her ear and turned her seed-pearl earring round and round. 'I called you back because learning about Hannah made me understand your obsession with Sam, because I wanted you

back with me and Emilie. It's what I've always wanted.'
She nodded towards their daughter. 'I gather you've got to
know each other again.' They both looked over at Emilie
at the far end of the garden; she was still inspecting the
vedettes and *sapeurs pompiers* moored along the bank under
the shade of Le Vert Galant. The light was hazy now as the
high roofs along the right bank sliced the sun in two, making
it glow and swell.

Jack took his father's blackthorn and, cupping both hands
over the swarthy knotted handle, rose from his seat and
walked over to Raphaëlle. She was still standing, under a
huge domed willow, her arms folded over her chest as she
stared at the cars and buses rumbling by across the river.
He placed a hand on her shoulder.

She did not move away. After a minute, she said:
'Remember the day we swam off Messanges and you
went under and almost lost consciousness? And your hand
gripped mine and we rose towards the surface and reached
the beach? And all those gulls circled above us, crying out
as we lay on our backs and the waves crashed about our
feet. Remember our hands gripping?'

'I remember,' he said. 'I should never have let go.'

She took his hand from her shoulder and held it in her
own, without turning around.

Jack's mouth was dry. There was still a hole somewhere
inside him, but he knew it was a hole no alcohol could fill.
A cut that nothing could salve. A rent that neither hand of
God nor man could ever stitch. A black gash. He tightened
his grasp on Raphaëlle's hand.

They stood beside the river, facing the soft yellow buildings of L'Institut and the high roof ateliers of the quays.
Church bells chimed the sixth hour past midday. They
watched the slate-grey, now jade, now copper waters of
the Seine roll by, a pale mackerel sky high above their
heads. And Jack remembered the sea down at Poul Gorm,
the pool between high rocks, where he'd first learned to

swim and where Sam had drowned. And Raphaëlle recalled the bottomless waves of Lac Léman where she'd so often glided through the water, buoyant and alive. And both of them noticed, perhaps at the same time, perhaps at different times, that a herring gull had perched on the iron-grid railing in front of them, wide-eyed, head erect, wings folding and unfolding.

'What do we do now?' asked Jack.

'We'll call Emilie and go swimming.' She smiled at him, then stretched her neck to face the evening sun as it sank down behind the grey-green roof of the Gare d'Orsay.

'Swimming?'

'Yes. The Deligny pool on Quai Voltaire, over there. It's open late on Fridays.' She pointed upriver. The air had thickened. The water moving through the bridge looked opaline now. And the trees began to fuse and fade then separate out in the dipping light.

'On the banks, on both sides of the river, there will grow all kinds of trees for food . . . The water for them flows from the sanctuary. Their fruit will be for food, and their leaves for healing.'

Ezekiel 47